PENGUIN BOOKS
DEAR WRITER IN THE WINDOW

GEORGELLE HIRLIMAN IS A WRITER IN AND OUT OF THE WINDOW, AND CAME BY HER WIT AND WISDOM THROUGH A VARIETY OF UNDERTAKINGS. SHE HAS WRITTEN AND PERFORMED ON RADIO, AND IS A PERFORMANCE ARTIST, AN ASTROLOGER, AND WRITES ESSAYS AND SHORT METAPHYSICAL FICTION. AS A FREELANCE JOURNALIST IN ALBUQUERQUE IN 1974 SHE INVESTIGATED THE MUCH-PUBLICIZED STORY OF FOUR CALIFORNIA BIKERS WHO WERE WRONGLY CONVICTED OF MURDER AND SENT TO DEATH ROW, AND SUBSEQUENTLY WROTE *THE HATE FACTORY* ABOUT THE SANTA FE PENITENTIARY RIOT.

SHE LIVES IN SANTA FE, NEW MEXICO, WITH TWO COCKATIELS, TWO FINCHES, AND ONE POCKET PARROT.

DEAR WRITER IN THE WINDOW

THE
WIT AND WISDOM
OF A SIDEWALK SAGE

GEORGELLE HIRLIMAN

PENGUIN BOOKS

PENGUIN BOOKS
Published by the Penguin Group
Viking Penguin, a division of Penguin Books USA Inc.,
375 Hudson Street, New York, New York 10014, U.S.A.
Penguin Books Ltd, 27 Wrights Lane,
London W8 5TZ, England
Penguin Books Australia Ltd, Ringwood,
Victoria, Australia
Penguin Books Canada Ltd, 10 Alcorn Avenue, Suite 300,
Toronto, Ontario, Canada M4V 3B2

Penguin Books (N. Z.) Ltd, 182-190 Wairau Road,
Auckland 10, New Zealand

Penguin Books Ltd, Registered Offices:
Harmondsworth, Middlesex, England

First published in Penguin Books 1992

1 3 5 7 9 10 8 6 4 2

LIBRARY OF CONGRESS CATALOGING IN PUBLICATION DATA
Hirliman, Georgelle
Dear writer in the window / Georgelle Hirliman.
p. cm.
ISBN 0 14 01.7043 X
1. Life—Miscellanea.   I. Title.
BD431.H485   1992
818'.5402—dc20   92–7784

Printed in the United States of America
Set in Gill Sans
Designed by Brian Mulligan

FOR MY DAUGHTER, HEATHER,
AND ALL MY SHELTERERS THROUGH THE STORM,
ESPECIALLY CHARLOTTE

for Jenny + Beth,

Best in life
Be with you —

Georgelee Herbener
3·14·93

CONTENTS

INTRODUCTION

A question demands an answer; the need of a demand for my writing brought *Dear Writer in the Window* into existence.

More than a decade ago, while looking out of a friend's storefront window in Manhattan, I had an idea: to write while sitting in the window, watching the grand mix of people pass by, and to be viewed while writing—even to have my writing-in-progress viewed and read. This seemed a perfect antidote to being cooped up in my author's "attic," creating in a world without feedback, applause, or human company. Writers, unless best-sellers, seldom know instant response to their work, seldom get accolades at the peak moment of performance the way actors, dancers, singers, and musicians do. "Applause" for the writer is delayed. Sometimes it doesn't arrive until death does. Sometimes it doesn't come at all. That's okay with many writers—the tower types, the introverts who write twenty-two hours a day, content in aloneness, happily hidden behind typewriter and research notes. But I am more a communicator than a tower writer, though I wasn't sure of that until I became The Writer in the Window.

Ten years after I had the image of writing in a storefront window (ten years spent writing in the tower), writer's block brought the idea back to me. I needed help—I needed a *demand* to inspire the words to flow. I certainly would have been motivated by a twenty-thousand-dollar, or even a five-hundred-dollar, demand, but such a commission was not forthcoming. Anyway, I was not inclined to try to tailor my subject or style to please a publisher. I had (and have) a stubborn will to write in my own way, and not even a serious case of writer's block, or bank-balance blues for that matter, could change my viewpoint. I needed a breakthrough to unlock my writing door, and the answer—write in a public window—flashed in my mind at exactly the right time. Santa Fe had an active, well-funded arts council that year, which was selecting artists for a summer street fest called Santa Fe City Streets. The council thought writing in a storefront window was an innovative idea and gave me the go-ahead to do it. Thanks to them, and to a creatively minded store owner who thought the idea charming, The Writer in the Window became a reality in the summer of 1984.

My original plan had been to start a novel in the window and tape the pages on the glass as I finished them. But as the day approached, I grew concerned: what if I got up there and didn't feel like writing the novel, if even the pressure of being in the window didn't unblock me? It could get boring for everyone. Again an answer flashed in my mind: Get audience participation. My first day in the window, I taped pad and pencil to the outside of the glass, next to this sign:

HELP CURE MY WRITER'S BLOCK.
JOT DOWN A TOPIC
YOU'D LIKE A PARAGRAPH WRITTEN ABOUT.

This was bingo. The questions poured in. Soon there was no time to write anything else. I'd not only invented a unique way of practicing the art of writing but tapped into people's need to talk about the big questions—what I call "why is the sky blue" ponderings—for which there is no forum in popular media today.

Over the next seven years, I became The Writer in the Window in dozens of stores in numerous cities. As I worked in different communities, I found that the questions in each of them demonstrated a different set of curiosities. Every city—and, in Manhattan, each neighborhood—had a distinctive slant on life. In New York City, there was the steamy blue-collar neighborhood around the *Village Voice* window; the very literate mixed stew of the Upper West Side around Shakespeare & Co.; the highly creative Greenwich Village neighborhood near Hudson Street Papers: they each had a unique flavor, but all of them were equally and grandly neurotic, a trait New Yorkers have worked to palatable perfection. In Santa Fe, the questions were mostly mystical and

"When will Mr. Right come along"–oriented, while in Portland, Oregon, they were more concerned with the state of our government and why we make such poor election choices.

In each place, the window became a living newspaper, a "window radio" that stimulated direct, live interaction with the written word! Exciting, always fascinating, it was for me a postgraduate course in writing. Because people often stood there waiting for their answers, there was no time to carve phrases into perfection. I had to "go in" and transcribe my immediate voice in one quick moment. Many questions were serious and inspiring, but my favorites were the nonsensical, even stupid, ones. They gave me the opportunity to make a mountain out of a molehill and practice being a storyteller.

A window reader recently suggested that The Writer in the Window idea would make a great party game, in the dictionary/fictionary/pictionary spirit. One person is the muse and poses a question for the rest of the group to answer, in writing. All the answers are given back to the muse, whose goal is to guess who wrote what. The mantle of muse then passes on to the next player. You, dear reader, might want to experiment with this idea. It might also be an excellent school tool.

The questions and answers in this book were collected from 1984 to 1991 in storefront windows in New York City, New Mexico, and Oregon. Because Santa Fe, New Mexico, is a major national and international tourist attraction, questions from there reflect global as well as local issues. There's something for, and *from,* almost everyone in this collection; and an unusual look at what humanity wonders about in these last challenging years of the twentieth century. The question asked most is: WHAT IS THE MEANING OF LIFE?

What's *your* answer?

—GEORGELLE HIRLIMAN,
THE WRITER IN THE WINDOW,
SANTA FE, NEW MEXICO,
MAY 1992

QUESTIONS AND ANSWERS ABOUT THE WRITER IN THE WINDOW

GALISTEO NEWS, SANTA FE, N.M.

TELL ME ABOUT YOURSELF, HUH?

I WAS BORN THE CHILD OF A BROTHER AND SISTER. IN BAKERSFIELD, CALIFORNIA, JUNE 11, 1936. QUICKLY, WITHIN ONE WEEK, I WAS ADOPTED. BY A GRADE-B MOVIE ACTRESS AND A FILM PRODUCER. THEY WERE BOTH ALCO-HOLICS, BUT OF A DIFFERENT SORT. SHE BINGED AND BECAME VIOLENT, TEARY-EYED, AND DANCEY. HE DRANK MORNING 'TIL NIGHT AND WAS GENTLE AND MELLOW. HE WAS THE PRODUCER OF THE CULT-CLASSIC FILM *REEFER MADNESS*. MOM WAS A BITCH, A GRADE-B JOAN CRAW-FORD. DAD WAS A MAN WHO LIKED A LOT OF SEX IN A LOT OF KINKY WAYS. HE DID NOT, HOWEVER, TRY ANY OF THIS OUT ON ME. OF THE TWO, DAD WAS BETTER TO ME

THAN MOM. MOM FORBADE ME TO BE AN ACTRESS, PULLED ME OUT OF DRESS REHEARSAL FOR MY MANHATTAN ACTING DEBUT, LITERALLY DRAGGING ME OUT OF THE THEATER BY MY HAIR, SCREAMING IN HER BEST CRAWFORD DRUNKEN TIRADE, "HELLSAFIAH, NO DAUGHTER OF MINE IS GOING TO BE AN ACTRESS." SO I BECAME A CHARACTER IN REAL LIFE. AT SIXTEEN, MOM KICKED ME OUT OF OUR NINE-ROOM MANHATTAN APARTMENT BECAUSE SHE'D OPENED A LETTER I'D WRITTEN TO A FRIEND AND TRANS-LATED MY TALE OF NECKING WITH A MARRIED MAN INTO THE SURETY THAT I'D "LOST MY CHERRY." AFTER FIFTEEN YEARS OF WAITRESSING, SECRETARYING, AND MODELING, I CAME FINALLY TO THE REALIZATION THAT THERE MUST BE SOMETHING I WAS TO DO IN LIFE THAT REFLECTED MORE OF MY VALUE AND TALENT AND INTELLIGENCE THAN THESE MENIAL OCCUPATIONS DID. IN A CHANGE-OF-LIFE SURGE, I MOVED TO SANTA FE, NEW MEXICO, WHERE I HAD TIME AND SPACE TO CONTEMPLATE MY INCLINATIONS AND TALENTS. SOON I REALIZED THAT WHAT I LOVED TO DO, AND ALWAYS DID DO, WAS COMMUNICATE. I TURNED THIS INTO A TRADE AND CRAFT BY WORKING AT KUNM RADIO, THE UNIVERSITY STATION IN ALBUQUERQUE. THERE I LEARNED TO INTERVIEW AND BE A NEWSPERSON. THIS LED ME TO COVER A MURDER TRIAL THAT TURNED OUT TO

BE, AS I THOUGHT IT WAS, A MISCARRIAGE OF JUSTICE, WHICH IN TURN LED TO A BOOK—MY FIRST—ON THE CRIMINAL JUSTICE SYSTEM (*THE WRONG PEOPLE*, NOT YET PUBLISHED) AND A SECOND BOOK, *THE HATE FACTORY*, ABOUT THE 1980 RIOT AT THE PENITENTIARY OF NEW MEXICO. BY THE TIME I FINISHED WRITING THESE TWO BOOKS, I KNEW IT WAS FUTILE TO THINK I OR ANYONE COULD EFFECT CHANGES IN THIS COUNTRY'S PRISON SYSTEM. INTO HIDING AND HEALING I WENT, HOPING FOR A NEW DIRECTION. FROM THIS, THE WRITER IN THE WINDOW EMERGED. I WAS MARRIED ONCE AND HAVE ONE DAUGHTER, WHO RECENTLY MARRIED A SHERIFF. I AM FIFTY-FIVE IN BODY TIME, YOUNG THOUGH ANCIENT IN SOUL TIME.

HUDSON STREET PAPERS, N.Y.C.

WHAT IS IT YOU ARE STRUGGLING WITH THAT YOU, AS A WRITER, WISH TO GIVE PEOPLE THROUGH YOUR WRITING?

HOW TO LIVE LIFE IN THE FULLEST, MOST HELPFUL WAY POSSIBLE, HELPFUL BOTH TO ME AND TO ALL. MY MAIN THRUST IN THESE REGARDS IS TO DO MY "TRUE WORK OF THE HEART" AND TO SUCCEED IN SUPPORTING

MY LIFE NEEDS THROUGH THAT WORK. I SEE THAT
PEOPLE ARE AFRAID OF INDEPENDENCE FROM THE SECURE
NINE-TO-FIVE WORK SYNDROME; THEY'RE SETTLING FOR
SLOW DEATH INSTEAD OF INVIGORATING, EVOLUTION-
PROVOKING, RISKY LIVING-BY-THE-WITS-TO-THE-TUNE-OF-
THE-INNER-MUSIC. IT'S THIS FEAR THAT I WISH TO ERASE
AND THIS LIVING-BY-THE-INNER-TUNE THAT I WISH TO
INSPIRE, IN MYSELF AND IN YOU, THROUGH MY WRITINGS.

■

SHAKESPEARE & CO., N.Y.C.

**WHAT DO YOU SEE WHEN YOU LOOK INTO
THE EYES OF PEOPLE THAT LOOK AT YOU?**

WHEN THEY *LET* ME LOOK INTO THEIR EYES, I SEE CURIOS-
ITY, BEFUDDLEMENT, APPRECIATION, A TWINKLE; IT VARIES.
BEFORE THEY LET ME CATCH THEIR EYES, I SEE CLOSURE,
QUESTIONING, SKEPTICISM. BUT USUALLY THE WRITINGS
WILL CREATE A SMILE, AND IF THEY DON'T, MY OWN SMILE
BREAKS THE SERIOUSNESS ON THEIR FACE, AND THEIR
CHEERY NATURE GRINS BACK. WHICH LEADS ME TO
BELIEVE THAT MOST HUMANS ARE OPEN TO "GOODWILL"
ONCE IT'S OFFERED BUT WARY OF BEING THE ONE TO
OFFER IT.

THE
MEANING
OF LIFE

THE LIVING BATCH BOOKSTORE, ALBUQUERQUE, N.M.

WHAT

IS THE

UNIVERSE

AND MORE—

WHAT IS THE

PURPOSE

OF IT

ALL?

THE UNIVERSE IS A POEM

WITH ONE THEME: EXPERIENCE.

(*UNI* = ONE; *VERSE* = POEM)

THE GAMUT, SANTA FE, N.M.

WHAT'S LIFE ALL ABOUT?
(Asked by an eleven-year-old)

EXPERIENCE

LEARNING

LOVING

CHANGE

■

THE VILLAGE VOICE, N.Y.C.

WHY DOES EVERYTHING SUCK SO MUCH, AND WHY DO YOU CARE?

BECAUSE EVERYTHING IS STILL IN THE STATE OF INFANCY.

■

HUDSON STREET PAPERS, N.Y.C.

IF WISHES WERE HORSES, WOULD BEGGARS REALLY RIDE?

IF WISHES WERE HORSES, WE'D BE TRAMPLED TO DEATH!

■

THE GAMUT, SANTA FE, N.M.

WHY IS THERE AIR?

AIR IS AN ENVELOPE THAT PROTECTS THE MESSAGE

OF OUR BEING.

GALISTEO NEWS, SANTA FE, N.M.

WHY TIME?

TIME IS A TEMPLATE WISDOM IS SQUEEZED THROUGH.

■

THE VILLAGE VOICE, N.Y.C.

**WHY IS PATIENCE A VIRTUE WHEN THE
WORLD MIGHT END TOMORROW?**

WHY RUIN TODAY WITH NEUROTIC RUSH?

■

HUDSON STREET PAPERS, N.Y.C.

WHY BOTHER?

IT'S THE MORE INTERESTING ALTERNATIVE.

■

THE GAMUT, SANTA FE, N.M.

**IS IT TRUE, AS THE ROMANS SAID, THAT "IN
VINO VERITAS" (IN WINE IS TRUTH)? CAN
TRUTH BE FOUND ALSO IN A
QUART OF COORS?**

CERTAINLY. TRUTH DWELLS EQUALLY IN COORS, COW
DUNG, MURDERERS, AND HUMANITY. AND AS WILLIAM
BLAKE SAID, "THROUGH THE PATH OF EXCESS LIES THE
ROAD TO WISDOM." HOW CAN YOU SEE THE LIGHT IF YOU
HAVEN'T SEEN THE DARK?

THE WIND CANNOT BE PERCEIVED BY SCIENTISTS. IT HITS YOU IN THE FACE, IT SLOWS YOU DOWN, IT BLOWS THE DUST AWAY. BUT THERE IS NOTHING PUSHING AIR, CAUSING WIND. GRAVITY CRUISING IN ON AIR DOES NOT CAUSE A FORCE AS STRONG AS WIND. WIND IS SO POORLY DEFINED IN BOOKS, IT IS REFERRED TO AS A "FORCE UNKNOWN" IN *THE PEOPLE'S ALMANAC*. WHAT IS THE AIR THAT HITS YOU IN THE FACE?

WIND IS THE MOVEMENT OF THE GASEOUS MIXTURE THAT ENVELOPS THE EARTH, THE BLOWING OF THE ETHERS CAUSED BY TEMPERATURE AND GEOGRAPHY. WIND IS THE EARTH SPIRIT RUFFLED BY THE EARTH HUMORS. THE GREEK ROOT FOR "WIND," *AER*, IS RELATED TO THE GREEK *AURA*, FOR BREATH, VAPOR, AND OF COURSE AURA ITSELF; AND THE ROOT OF "WIND," *WE*, IS *VATI* IN SANSKRIT, WHICH IS RELATED TO THE WORD "*NIRVANA*." THUS, THE AIR THAT HITS YOU IN THE FACE IS AKIN TO THE ZEN MASTER WHO SMACKS YOU ON THE HEAD WHEN YOU FUSS AND TWIDGET INSTEAD OF SITTING FOCUSED ON BREATH OR MANTRA (BOTH OF THESE WORDS ARE ALSO ASSOCIATED WITH *AIR* AND *WIND*). WIND IS NATURE'S REMINDER THAT THE MOST SOLID MATTER CAN BE DESTROYED BY THE FORCE OF THE ETHERIC AURA OF THE WORLD.

THE GAMUT, SANTA FE, N.M.

HOW CAN WE HEAL THE PAIN OF GOD?

HEAL YOUR OWN PAIN. THEN TRY TO HEAL SOMEONE ELSE'S. KEEP ON HEALIN'.

■

THE GAMUT, SANTA FE, N.M.

WHO OR WHAT IS GOD?
(Asked by a seven-year-old)

GOD IS THE NAME WE GIVE TO THE INTELLIGENCE THAT CREATED THE UNIVERSE AND ALL IN IT; GOD IS THE NAME WE GIVE TO THE ENERGY THAT MAKES UP OUR ENTIRE BODY AND THE BODY OF ALL THAT EXISTS.

COLLEGE OF SANTA FE, SANTA FE, N.M.

ANALYZE THE STATEMENT: "RELIGION DOES NOT TEACH LOVE, IT REPLACES LOVE." I FEEL THAT THE LOVE OF THE HUMAN RACE IS AN ABSOLUTE NECESSITY BUT THAT LOVE OF AN ABSTRACT STUNTS THAT LOVE INTO SOMETHING THAT CANNOT BE USED; ONE BEGINS LOVING THE CONCEPT ONLY. OPINION?

I AGREE. "RELIGION DOES NOT TEACH LOVE, IT REPLACES LOVE" EXPRESSES THE "SIN" OF RELIGION, THE NOTHINGNESS RELIGION HAS BECOME. FEW, IF ANY, RELIGIONS TODAY EXPRESS/TEACH/EMBRACE LOVE AND RESPECT FOR *LIFE* AND THE WAY OF LIFE, OR HONOR THE MOST PRIMAL OF HUMAN NEEDS, SEX, AS A SACRAMENT; OR ENJOYMENT OF LIFE'S PLEASURES AS SERVICE AND THE CULTIVATION OF INDIVIDUALITY AS DUTY. ONCE, THE AMERICAN INDIANS PRACTICED IN THIS MANNER, UNITING THEMSELVES WITH UNIVERSAL FORCES, AND, TO SOME EXTENT, SO DID THE TANTRICS IN TIBET. BUT THE LAST LORE OF LIFE-AS-RELIGION RESTS WITH MATRIARCHAL LEGENDS OF AN UNRECORDED TIME. HUMANITY, NOT CONCEPT, NEEDS OUR LOVE AND HONORING, I AGREE.

GALISTEO NEWS, SANTA FE, N.M.

WHICH CAME FIRST—THE SUFI OR THE EGG?

MOST OF THE TIME, THE SUFI WAS LATE TO BREAKFAST BECAUSE OF ALL THE MORNING RITUALS, SO MOST OF THE TIME THE EGG ARRIVED AT THE TABLE BEFORE THE SUFI DID. AND ANYWAY, THE EGG ALWAYS COMES BEFORE THE SUFI OR THE HINDU OR ANY BEING ENSCONCED IN RELIGIOUS DEVOTIONS: THE EGG OF CONCEPTION PRECEDES THE CONCEPTION OF RITUAL.

■

HUDSON STREET PAPERS, N.Y.C.

WHAT IS CONSTANT?

CHANGE.

■

THE GAMUT, SANTA FE, N.M.

IS GOD A VERB?

YES, ACTUALLY. NOW HUMANITY JUST HAS TO DISCOVER IT.

THE VILLAGE VOICE, N.Y.C.

WHY DO WOMEN TRUST RELIGIOUS TEACHINGS WHEN THERE ISN'T A SINGLE RELIGION THAT TREATS THEM AS EQUAL TO MEN?
(Asked by a man)

WHERE ELSE CAN A WOMAN WHO DESIRES A SPIRITUAL PRACTICE GO BUT TO THE ESTABLISHED CITADELS OF SUCH PRACTICES? SHE HAS BEEN IN THE SERVANT POSITION AND FORBIDDEN ESTABLISHMENT OF HER OWN RELIGIOUS WAY IN THIS LONG PATERNAL ERA. I THINK A WOMAN WOULD NEVER SET UP A "RELIGION" OR ISSUE DOGMATIC RULES. WOMEN WOULD BRING A FREER FORM OF SPIRITUAL PRACTICE, A DO-IT-YOURSELF-AS-YOU-GO SPIRITUALITY THAT SAW "GOD" AS THE ESSENCE OF EVERYTHING AND GENDERLESS. MAYBE THIS IS WHY WE HAVE NO FEMALE RELIGIOUS *LEADERS*—"WOMAN" SIMPLY DOESN'T AGREE WITH THE CONCEPT OF "SPIRITUAL LEADER." AND THOSE OF US WOMEN WHO DO GO TO GURUS FOR TECHNIQUE NEED TO BE FILTERING THE TEACHINGS THROUGH OUR OWN SIFTER, OUR INTUITIVE MIND, LETTING IT TEMPER THE PATRIARCHAL MANDATES. ACTUALLY, EVERYONE NEEDS TO DO THAT WITH THE SPIRITUAL TEACHINGS THAT ARE IMBIBED. WHY SWALLOW THE STUFF WHOLE? CHEW, DIGEST, ASSIMILATE, TRANSFORM.

HUDSON STREET PAPERS, N.Y.C.

DID I MAKE A MISTAKE IN CHICAGO?

THE ONLY MISTAKES WE MAKE ARE THESE:

THE MISTAKE OF NOT EXPERIENCING THE MOMENTS

OFFERED.

THE MISTAKE OF ATTACHMENT.

THE MISTAKE OF NOT LOVING.

DID YOU MAKE A MISTAKE IN CHICAGO?

■

THE GAMUT, SANTA FE, N.M.

WHY DON'T ALL PEOPLE BELIEVE IN JESUS CHRIST AS THEIR SAVIOR?

BECAUSE ALL PEOPLE ARE UNIQUE, EACH AND EVERY ONE
FACETED AND GEARED IN A WAY NO OTHER IS; AND FOR
EACH AND EVERY ONE OF THESE "ALL PEOPLE," THERE IS A
DIFFERENT PATHWAY TO "GOD." SOME FIND THAT PATH-
WAY THROUGH JESUS, SOME THROUGH BUDDHA, SOME
THROUGH SHIVA, SOME THROUGH AGNOSTICISM. TRUTH
AND GOD ARE MULTI-RENDERED THINGS.

GALISTEO NEWS, SANTA FE, N.M.

WHY DO YOU ENJOY PLAYING GOD WITH YOUR ANSWERS WHEN "ALL THINGS THAT PERTAIN TO LIFE AND GODLINESS" ARE WRITTEN IN GOD'S WORD (THE BIBLE)? WRITER ON THE SIDEWALK—SHADDUP.

WE'RE ALL BIBLES, AND ALL I'M PLAYING IS THE "KINGDOM OF GOD" WITHIN ME. AND YOU?

■

GALISTEO NEWS, SANTA FE, N.M.

IT'S MY THIRTY-FIRST BIRTHDAY. WHAT SHOULD I KNOW BY NOW?

BY THIRTY-ONE, YOU "SHOULD" KNOW HOW TO FACE LIFE AND ITS DENSE DIFFICULTY WITH THE FULL FORCE OF YOUR WILL TO LIVE, HOW TO PUSH THROUGH ALL OBSTA-CLES THAT STAND IN YOUR WAY. AT THIRTY-ONE, THE NATURE OF YOUR PERSONALITY SHOULD BE KNOWN TO YOU, AND THE TRUE, INNER NATURE OF YOUR SELF SHOULD BE *BECOMING* APPARENT. THE FIRST GLIMMER OF DISSATISFACTION WITH ENDEAVORS NOT IN SYNC WITH YOUR BLOSSOMING SELF SHOULD BE BEING FELT BY YOU, SO THE SUBSEQUENT CHANGE IN LIFEWAY CAN BEGIN. AT THIRTY-ONE, YOU SHOULD KNOW HOW TO MAKE LOVE WITH A PARTNER: THAT IS, THE TECHNIQUES REQUIRED TO GIVE YOU AND YOUR PARTNER THE BEST EXPERIENCE AND THE OPENNESS NECESSARY FOR FEELINGS TO FLOW

BETWEEN YOU. AT THIRTY-ONE, YOU SHOULD BE ABLE TO PAY YOUR RENT AND PROVIDE FOR YOUR NEEDS. AT THIRTY-ONE, YOU SHOULD KNOW THE TIME HAS COME TO FIND YOUR TRUE WORK, YOUR TRUE "RELIGION," AND A TRUE PARTNERING.

■

HUDSON STREET PAPERS, N.Y.C.

IF LIFE IS A STAGE, WHY DO WE TAKE IT SO SERIOUSLY?

BECAUSE IT REQUIRES METHOD ACTING.

■

GALISTEO NEWS, SANTA FE, N.M.

WHY IS IT THAT SINCE I'M A PISCES, PEOPLE COME TO ME FOR HELP, WHEN I'M MORE LOST AND CONFUSED THAN THEY ARE?
—"Lost and Dazed"

DEAR COMPASSIONATE WATER MAIDEN WHO IS LOST AND DAZED:

YOU HAVE GREAT EMOTIONAL DEPTH AND EMPATHY IN YOUR PERSONALITY THROUGH BEING A PISCES. BECAUSE YOU SUFFER SO MUCH FROM YOUR OWN EXISTENTIAL ANGST, YOU HAVE SYMPATHY AND CONNECTION WITH OTHERS' SUFFERING. RELAX, AND GIVE WHAT COMFORT YOU CAN. YOU'LL RECEIVE WHAT YOU PUT OUT: PISCES' KEYNOTE IS "SERVE OR SUFFER."

GALISTEO NEWS, SANTA FE, N.M.

DO THE SIGNS OF THE ZODIAC HAVE AS MUCH INFLUENCE OVER PEOPLE AS WE THINK?

IT ISN'T THAT THE SIGNS INFLUENCE US; IT'S THAT THE SIGNS *DESCRIBE* OUR REACTION TO INFLUENCES SUR-ROUNDING OUR LIVES. THIS IS WHAT ASTROLOGY IS ABOUT: CHARACTER DESCRIPTION, AND WAYS AND MEANS FOR DEVELOPING THIS CHARACTER INTO ITS BEST FLOW-ERING.

■

HUDSON STREET PAPERS, N.Y.C.

WHY IS THERE ANYTHING RATHER THAN NOTHING AT ALL?

AFTER TIMELESS EONS OF NOTHINGNESS, *ANYTHING* SEEMED A BETTER IDEA.

■

THE GAMUT, SANTA FE, N.M.

HOW DO YOU DISTINGUISH THE TRUE PROPHETIC VOICE FROM THAT OF AN IRRITATED CRANK?

LISTEN WITH YOUR PROPHETIC EARS.

CRANKS MAKE A LOT OF NOISE.

B. DALTON, N.Y.C.

WHAT IS THE TRUE MEANING OF RELIGION?

"RELIGION" MEANS *UNION, COMMUNION WITH THE ABSO-LUTE ESSENCE OF ALL.* THAT'S MY DEFINITION. *AMERICAN HERITAGE DICTIONARY* DESCRIBES THE MEANING THUSLY: "THE EXPRESSION OF MAN'S BELIEF IN, AND REVERENCE FOR, A SUPERHUMAN POWER RECOGNIZED AS THE CRE-ATOR AND GOVERNOR OF THE UNIVERSE" (FROM *RELIGIO = BOND BETWEEN MAN AND THE GODS*). THE PROBLEMS WE THINK OF WHEN WE SPEAK OF "RELIGION" AS A "DIRTY" WORD ARE EXPLAINED IN THE ROOT OF THE WORD: *RE =* BACK + *LIGARE =* TO BIND, FASTEN. THUS HAS RELIGION BECOME A *BINDING* RATHER THAN A REVERENCING AND RECOGNIZING OF UNIVERSALS. WE MUST MAKE OUR OWN RELIGION, EACH FOR ONE'S SELF, M'THINKS.

■

GALISTEO NEWS, SANTA FE, N.M.

WHERE DO I FIND MYSELF?

INSIDE, WHERE YOU ARE NOW.

IN THE EYES OF A LOVING FRIEND, WHERE YOU LONG TO BE.

■

HUDSON STREET PAPERS, N.Y.C.

WHAT DO YOU FEEL THE MOST IMPORTANT IDEA OF THIS CENTURY/ALL TIME IS?

"GOD" DWELLS WITHIN YOU AS YOU.

SHAKESPEARE & CO., N.Y.C.

IS THERE GOD? IF SO, WHY IS HE SO MEAN?

YES, THERE IS THIS THING WE INSIST ON MAKING A "HE" AND CALLING "GOD." *IT*, THIS ESSENTIAL ENERGY THAT IS THE BASE AND CAUSE AND ESSENCE OF ALL, EXISTS WITHIN EVERY ATOM OF YOUR BEING AND MINE AND THIS TYPE YOU'RE READING. HOWEVER, IT HAS GOTTEN SO BURIED IN THE BODY OF EXISTENCE, IT HAS FORGOTTEN ITS *ESSENCE NATURE* AND IDENTIFIES WITH THIS PHYSICAL WORLD. THUS, SINCE THERE IS NO GUIDE DANCE AROUND BUT THE NEUROTIC MIND-MAZES OF EGOED INTELLECTS, HUMANITY GOES ON LIKE STALE M&M'S, UNABLE TO FEEL THE BLISS-PRODUCING CHOCOLATE NUGGET. CHANT CHOCOLATE OHMMMS TO WAKEN "GOD."

■

GALISTEO NEWS, SANTA FE, N.M.

WHY IS THE UNITY OF ALL THINGS SO HARD FOR THE ISOLATED COMPONENTS TO PERCEIVE?

ALL SEEING IS FROM THE SEER'S POSITIONAL POINT OF VIEW. DOES NOT THE UNITY FORGET THE ISOLATED COMPONENT TOO? HOW DO WE GET UNITY AND ISOLATED ACQUAINTED? INTERACT, MAKE WAVES, PASS THE WORD ALONG THE ELECTRONS.

B. DALTON, N.Y.C.

IS THE POET OR THE PHILOSOPHER MORE CORRECT IN INTERPRETING REALITY?

THE POET EXPRESSES THE SOUL OF REALITY; THE PHILOSO-PHER EXPRESSES THE MIND OF REALITY. BOTH ARE CORRECT, IN THEIR GIVEN SPHERES.

■

GALISTEO NEWS, SANTA FE, N.M.

IF, IN THE MIDST OF CHARITY, THE RECEIVER IS PATRONIZED, IS THE CHARITABLE ACT STILL WORTHWHILE?

THE ROOT OF THE WORD "CHARITY" IS THE LATIN *CARITAS* = LOVE, FROM *CARUS* = DEAR. SO IF IN THE MIDST OF YOUR CHARITY YOU FEEL ANYTHING LESS THAN LOVE FOR THE DEARNESS OF THE CAUSE OR PERSON TO WHOM YOU GIVE YOUR CHARITY, CHARITY IT IS NOT.

■

SHAKESPEARE & CO., N.Y.C.

HOW DO I KNOW IF MY INSTINCT IS RIGHT?

TRY IT OUT.

■

STAGHORN, N.Y.C.

WHY ISN'T THE MEANING OF LIFE MORE EASILY OBTAINABLE?

GOD LOVES A GOOD GAME OF HIDE-AND-SEEK.

CARDS & SUCH, FOREST HILLS, N.Y.

TOPIC SUGGESTION:
THE QUEST FOR INDESCRIBABLE JOY

. . . BEGINS WITH SEX, MIDDLES WITH CREATIVE ENDEAVOR,

AND IS PERFECTED IN EXPERIENCE OF THE SPIRIT IN ALL.

■

GALISTEO NEWS, SANTA FE, N.M.

HOW DO WE KNOW THAT WE KNOW?

THE SILENT PLACE IN THE HEART CAVE MURMURS ASSENT.

■

THE VILLAGE VOICE, N.Y.C.

"O, BUT HOW MANY SCORES OF SIBYLS," HE
THINKS, "WOULD IT TAKE TO REVEAL THE
TRUTH OF A SPHINX?"

"AND HOW MANY RULES OF THE RUNES," SHE PONDERS,

"MUST A SOUL REALLY KNOW TO QUIT ITS WANDERS?"

■

GALISTEO NEWS, SANTA FE, N.M.

WHY OH WHY CAN WE NOT ALWAYS
FLY SO HIGH?

WE'RE MADE TO USE LEGS AND ARMS, NOT WINGS. HENCE

FLYING IS EXPENSIVE: ONE WAY OR THE OTHER, THE

MEANS MUST BE MANUFACTURED. NOT THAT THIS IS BAD;

IT'S GOOD TO GET A BIRD'S-EYE VIEW FROM TIME TO TIME.

BUT IT'S THE ARMS AND LEGS THAT MOTOR US ALONG

EARTH'S EXPERIENCES, AND THE THOROUGHNESS THESE MEANS OF TRAVEL ENTAIL MUST BE EMBRACED TO GET THE FULL EARTH MESSAGE.

■

STAGHORN, N.Y.C.

IS LIFE, IN FACT, A BOWL OF CHERRIES?

YES, AND, LIKE CHERRIES, FULL OF PITS, WITH A TENDENCY TO CAUSE DIARRHEA WHEN OVERINDULGED IN.

■

STAGHORN, N.Y.C.

HOW CAN THERE BE A GOD WHEN THERE IS SO MUCH UNMITIGATED SUFFERING IN THE WORLD?

THE EASTERN TRANSCENDENTAL VIEWPOINT PROVIDES THE BEST ANSWER I'VE HEARD FOR THIS. MY FAVORITE TEACHER TOLD THIS QUINTESSENTIAL STORY ABOUT WHAT'S BECOME OF GOD:

TWO BROTHERS WERE FIGHTING OVER TERRITORY, SO FIERCELY THAT THE ANGELIC GUARDIANS OF THE PROVINCE APPEALED TO VISHNU, THE PRESERVER ASPECT OF THE HINDU THREEFOLD GODHEAD, TO HELP. VISHNU AGREED AND CAME TO EARTH AS AN EXQUISITE WOMAN, OVER WHOM THE BROTHERS FOUGHT, AS WAS VISHNU'S PLAN. ONE OF THE BROTHERS WAS KILLED, THUS ENDING

THE LAND WAR, AND THE SURVIVOR ASKED FOR VISHNU-AS-WOMAN'S HAND IN MARRIAGE. SHE AGREED, AND SOON VISHNU GOT CAUGHT IN THE JOYS OF JEWELS AND BEAUTY AND FORGOT HER TRUE STATE OF BEING: THE ASPECT OF GOD THAT KEEPS LIFE GOING. IT TOOK SHIVA, THE FACE OF GOD THAT DESTROYS ILLUSION, TO SHAKE VISHNU OUT OF HIS DANCE WITH THE SENSES, BACK INTO REMEMBRANCE OF HIS GOD NATURE.

SO IT IS ON EARTH: GOD, DWELLING IN ALL MANIFESTATION, BE IT PEOPLE, ROCK, OR AIR, IS THEREBY, AND BY NOW, COVERED WITH THE DIRT OF LIFE—MUCH LIKE AN M&M CANDY, SO COATED WITH SUGAR, THE CHOCOLATE INSIDE CAN'T MELT IN THE HANDS OF LOVE. THIS IS WHY IT IS SAID THAT JUST TO CHANT THE NAMES OF GOD IN THESE DIFFICULT, INERTIA-PRONE TIMES IS ENOUGH TO KEEP ONE OUT OF PURE HELL, FOR THE KERNEL OF "ESSENTIAL STUFF" WITHIN US ALL MUST BE CONTINUALLY REMINDED OF ITSELF IF IT IS TO SHINE THROUGH ALL THE SHIT WE'VE PILED ON THROUGH THE AGES. THIS MEANS THAT OUR SELF-LOATHING IS NOT ONLY PERSONAL PSYCHOLOGY BUT THAT THE GODHEAD WITHIN EACH OF US IS A LITTLE PISSED AT ITSELF FOR LETTING ITS EXPERIENCE IN CREATION GET SO OUT OF HAND. WE ALL KNOW HUMANS MAKE MISTAKES; MAYBE GOD DID TOO.

THE VILLAGE VOICE, N.Y.C.

**MY NAME IS CHRIS. I THINK I'M THE SECOND
SON OF GOD. CAN I PROVE IT? SHOW ME
HOW . . . OR HELP ME PROVE IT.
THIS IS NOT SACRILEGIOUS.**

YOU'RE ACTUALLY THE SIX BILLIONTH CHILD OF GOD:
THIS IS NO SACRILEGE.

THE GAMUT, SANTA FE, N.M.

WHERE IS THE END OF THE UNIVERSE?
(Asked by a ten-year-old boy)

THE END OF THE UNIVERSE SURROUNDS YOU, AS DOES
THE BEGINNING. YOU ARE JUST SO INVOLVED IN THE
"NOW" THAT YOU DO NOT TUNE IN TO THE "END." EXIS-
TENCE, IT IS SAID, IS A SIMULTANEOUS EVENT: YOU ARE
LIVING PAST, PRESENT, AND FUTURE AT THIS MOMENT,
BUT YOUR CONSCIOUSNESS IS DIVIDED BY WALLS OF TIME
AND MATTER. THEREFORE, WHAT YOU DO AND THINK
"TODAY" HAS AN IMMEDIATE EFFECT ON THE "END" OF
THE UNIVERSE.

HUDSON STREET PAPERS, N.Y.C.

WHAT IS MY CAT THINKING ABOUT?
(Asked by a twelve-year-old girl)

LIFE AS A LION EONS AGO.

THE GAMUT, SANTA FE, N.M.

HOW DO YOU GET TO BE BEAUTIFUL?
(Asked by Amanda, almost six)

FROM THE INSIDE OUT.

■

THE GAMUT, SANTA FE, N.M.

WHY ISN'T EVERYONE PSYCHIC?
(Asked by an eight-year-old)

THEY ARE, THEY JUST HAVEN'T WOKEN UP TO THEIR CON-
NECTION WITH ALL AND EVERYTHING.

■

GALISTEO NEWS, SANTA FE, N.M.

IS SILENCE A NOISE?
IF SO, CAN YOU HEAR IT?

SILENCE IS NOT A NOISE, BUT IT HAS

A PROFOUND SOUND.

■

THE GAMUT, SANTA FE, N.M.

WHY IS THE SKY BLUE?

WHEN THE FREE-FLOATING INTRINSIC PARTICLES AND
WAVES THAT CONSTITUTE ALL OF EXISTENCE MEET A
DENSER, TOUGHER, TIGHTER GROUP OF PARTICLES AND
WAVES, SUCH AS THE ATMOSPHERE THAT SURROUNDS OUR
PLANET, THE ENERGY CAUSED AND DISCHARGED BY THEIR
MEETING PRODUCES MANY EFFECTS, MANY WONDROUS

EARTHLY AND HEAVENLY BEAUTIES ABOUT WHICH WE HUMANS COMPOSE GREAT HYMNS AND PROSE OF PRAISE. ONE OF THESE EFFECTS IS COLOR.

■

GALISTEO NEWS, SANTA FE, N.M.

WHY IS NO MORE POWERFUL THAN YES?

BECAUSE "NO" IS A FORCE THAT STOPS. IN A WORLD OF CONSTANT MOTION, OF CONTINUAL YES, THE NO THAT STOPS PRODUCES A FREEZING SHOCK OF SHIPWRECKING ICEBERGS AND UNINHABITABLE GLACIERS.

■

GALISTEO NEWS, SANTA FE, N.M.

WHY DOES MAN CONTINUALLY SCREAM AT THE DARKNESS RATHER THAN LIGHT A CANDLE?!

MY DEAR, HE'S SIMPLY TRYING TO GET *SOMEONE* TO HEAR HIM AND HAND HIM A MATCH!

■

GALISTEO NEWS, SANTA FE, N.M.

WHY IS IT THAT MOST PEOPLE DON'T WANT TO DRINK THE WATER UNTIL THE WELL RUNS DRY? — Mr. L.

YO, DUDE, MR. L., MORE IS THE MANTRA, FURTHER IS THE FATE, GREENER GRASS IS THE GOAL. DOSE OF REALITY, MAN.

GALISTEO NEWS, SANTA FE, N.M.

**WHY DO THE STARS SHINE AT NIGHT AND
NOT DURING THE DAY?**
(Asked by a seven-year-old)

THEY'RE STARS FROM ANOTHER COUNTRY, AND OUR VERY
OWN SUPERSTAR, SOL, THE SUN, IS JEALOUS OF HIS
CENTER-STAGE POSITION, HENCE LETS NO OTHER LIGHT
SHARE THE STAGE. THE MOON, HOWEVER, USED TO PLAY-
ING SECOND FIDDLE TO A BRIGHTER MAGNITUDE, IS
HAPPY TO HAVE THESE VISITING LIGHTS DECORATE HER
STAGE.

■

GALISTEO NEWS, SANTA FE, N.M.

**WHAT IS THE ANSWER TO LIFE,
THE UNIVERSE, AND EVERYTHING?**

YES.

■

GALISTEO NEWS, SANTA FE, N.M.

WHAT IS DIFFERENT?

EACH MOMENT.

GALISTEO NEWS, SANTA FE, N.M.

WHY ARE THE LITTLEST THINGS IN LIFE
SO IMPORTANT?

HAVEN'T YOU NOTICED THAT LIFE IS MADE UP OF THE SMALLEST DETAILS? IT'S THE LITTLE MOLECULES THAT MAKE THE BIG PLANET, THE ARRANGEMENT OF THE SMALLEST CRYSTALS THAT MAKES THE RELATIVELY LARGE SNOWFLAKE, THE LITTLE WAY YOU CURL YOUR MOUTH IN ANGER THAT RUINS THE DAY FOR YOUR LOVER.

■

GALISTEO NEWS, SANTA FE, N.M.

THERE SEEM TO BE THOUSANDS OF PHILOSOPHERS THROUGHOUT TIME WHO HAVE CLAIMED TO EXPLAIN WHY, YET NONE OF THEM REALLY HAVE. WHY CAN'T WE FIGURE OUT OUR REASONS OR REASON FOR EXISTENCE HERE ON EARTH? P.S. WHY DO OUR DRYERS EAT ONLY ONE SOCK FROM A PAIR?

WE'RE INFANTS AS A SPECIES, WE HUMANS, AND OUR PHILOSOPHERS ARE JUST A LITTLE AHEAD OF THE REST OF US. WE'VE HAD NEITHER THE MENTAL CAPACITY NOR THE SCIENTIFIC TOOLS TO PUT THE ENTIRE PICTURE TOGETHER. NOW WE DO, AND OUR SCIENTISTS ARE BECOMING OUR SAGES. THEY ARE DISCOVERING IN THE PHYSICAL UNIVERSE PROOF AND EXAMPLE OF WHAT THE TRANSCENDENTAL PHILOSOPHIES HAVE IMAGINED FOR

CENTURIES. IN TRYING TO EXPLAIN "WHY" WE EXIST, MOST PHILOSOPHERS HAVE PROPOSED THAT THERE IS *PURPOSE* AND PROCEEDED TO EXPOUND UPON THE VIRTUES OF THAT PURPOSE. BUT IF THEY, AND WE WHO LISTENED TO THEM, HAD HEEDED THE TRUE MEANING OF *REASON*, WE WOULD HAVE LOOKED MORE FOR *HOW* IT ALL WORKED, AND GUIDED OUR LIVES ACCORDINGLY. THIS, I THINK, IS HAPPENING NOW. SINCE THE ORIGIN OF "REASON" COMES FROM THE ROOT *AR* = TO FIT TOGETHER, MOST LIKELY OUR DRYERS EAT ONLY ONE SOCK FROM A PAIR BECAUSE THEY HAVE NO REASONING ABILITY!

■

GALISTEO NEWS, SANTA FE, N.M.

WHAT IS THE DIFFERENCE BETWEEN TRUTH AND HONESTY?

WITHOUT PEEKING, I'D SAY THE DIFFERENCE IS THAT TRUTH IS OBJECTIVE AND STATIC, MORE A NOUN, WHILE HONESTY IS SUBJECTIVE AND ACTIVE, A VERB. WE TELL THE TRUTH ABOUT AN EVENT AND ARE HONEST ABOUT OUR FEELINGS. *AMERICAN HERITAGE DICTIONARY* AGREES WITH ME TOTALLY ABOUT TRUTH AND ESSENTIALLY ABOUT HONESTY. HONESTY, IT SAYS, IS A CONDITION, "THE CAPACITY OR CONDITION OF BEING HONEST." "HONEST" IS DEFINED AS "NOT LYING, CHEATING, STEALING OR TAK-

ING UNFAIR ADVANTAGE." THE DICTIONARY CALLS "HON-
ESTY" A NOUN, BUT IT IS STILL A SUBJECTIVE NOUN, AND
I THINK IT HAS A RATHER ACTIVE DEFINITION. "TRUTH,"
ON THE OTHER HAND, IS DEFINED MORE STATICALLY AND
ALSO CALLED A NOUN. TRUTH, THE DICTIONARY SAYS, IS
"CONFORMITY TO KNOWLEDGE, FACT, ACTUALITY OR
LOGIC. FIDELITY TO AN ORIGINAL OR STANDARD. REALITY.
A STATEMENT PROVEN TO BE OR ACCEPTED AS TRUE." I
THINK TRUTH IS HARD IF NOT IMPOSSIBLE TO FIND, BUT
HONESTY IS AVAILABLE TO US RIGHT NOW.

GALISTEO NEWS, SANTA FE, N.M.

WHY DOES A FLOWER BLOOM?

BECAUSE FLOWERS LOVE TO BE FULL AND OPEN TO ALL
WHO NEED THEM.

STAGHORN, N.Y.C.

CAN A PERSON BENEFIT AND FIND
SOMETHING GOOD FROM
A PERSONAL TRAGEDY?

IF ONE COULDN'T, LIFE WOULD BE A WASTE, WOULDN'T
IT, GIVEN THE CERTAINTY OF PERSONAL TRAGEDY ENTER-
ING EVERYONE'S SPHERE AT LEAST ONCE? PERSONAL
TRAGEDY IS ONE OF THE BETTER TEACHERS IN LIFE.

HUDSON STREET PAPERS, N.Y.C.

WILL I TRULY FIND MY INNER SELF SOON?

BETWEEN THE OUTER AND THE INNER, WHERE IS THE SEPARATION?

■

COLLEGE OF SANTA FE, SANTA FE, N.M.

HOW DO YOU LEARN TO LIVE WITH YOURSELF AFTER YOU DISCOVER YOU'RE YOUR OWN WORST ENEMY?!

YOU LEARN TO LOVE YOUR ENEMY; THAT'S WHY CHARITY BEGINS AT HOME!

■

THE GAMUT, SANTA FE, N.M.

WHY DOES ONE HAVE TO TURN THIRTY?

TO EXPRESS WHAT WAS LEARNED IN THE TWENTIES AND DEVELOP THE CREATIVE TALENTS THAT WILL FIND ONE'S POWER PLACE IN THE FORTIES. NUMEROLOGICALLY SPEAK- ING, THE TWENTIES (2) ARE FOR RECEIVING INFO; THE THIRTIES (3) ARE FOR EXPRESSING AND CREATING; THE FORTIES (4) ARE FOR ESTABLISHING FOUNDATIONS OF PER- SONAL POWER; THE FIFTIES (5) ARE FOR FREE EXPERIENC- ING; THE SIXTIES (6) ARE FOR SHARING WISDOM GAINED THROUGH THE LIFE'S WORK; THE SEVENTIES (7) ARE FOR INTROSPECTION AND SPIRITUAL REFLECTION. THE EIGHT- IES AND NINETIES ARE SO SELDOM REACHED WITH FULL

AWARENESS THAT WHAT YOU DO WITH THEM IS UP TO YOU. BUT YOU'RE STILL WORRIED ABOUT THE *THIRTIES!* YOU'VE ONLY BEGUN TO KNOW WHAT LIVING IS ABOUT.

■

SHAKESPEARE & CO., N.Y.C.

IS THAT ALL THERE IS?

IT'S UP TO YOU.

■

THE GAMUT, SANTA FE, N.M.

WHAT IS SADNESS? DOES IT HAVE A FUNCTION?

SADNESS IS THE FLOOD OF FEELINGS THAT AWAKENS YOU TO THE FACT THAT YOU HAVE HAD ENOUGH, THAT YOU ARE WEARY, TOO FULL OF LIFE'S FRUSTRATIONS TO FEEL ANY SUNSHINE. THE FUNCTION OF SADNESS IS THE FUNCTION OF FEELINGS: TO ALERT YOU TO YOUR REACTION TO THE SITUATION CAUSING IT AND TO MAKE YOU EXPERIENCE TOTALLY HOW THE SITUATION AFFECTS YOU. SADNESS IS THE SOLUTION IN WHICH HUMANITY DISSOLVES ANGER AND GROWS COMPASSION. ("SAD" [ACCORDING TO *AMERICAN HERITAGE DICTIONARY*]: "LOW IN SPIRIT; DEJECTED; SORROWFUL; UNHAPPY. . . . OLD ENGLISH *SAED,* SATED, WEARY.")

GALISTEO NEWS, SANTA FE, N.M.

WHAT IS THE THERAPEUTIC VALUE OF
SINGING IN THE SHOWER?

CLEARING OUT THE INNER WHILE SHOWERING OFF THE
OUTER DIRT. THE THROAT CHAKRA IS SAID TO BE THE
CLEARING-OUT CENTER; SINGING AND CHANTING, THEN,
ARE THE MECHANISMS FOR PSYCHIC CLEANSING.

GALISTEO NEWS, SANTA FE, N.M.

WHY DOES VIOLENCE EXIST WHERE THERE
COULD BE LOVE?

ALLERGIC REACTION TO DIFFERENCES.

GALISTEO NEWS, SANTA FE, N.M.

WHY ARE PEOPLE SO AFRAID OF DEATH? WHY
AREN'T THEY HAPPY THAT THEY HAD THE
CHANCE TO LIVE?

PEOPLE ARE AFRAID OF DEATH BECAUSE THEY HAVE BEEN
TAUGHT THAT IT IS A FINAL ENDING.

PEOPLE ARE AFRAID OF DEATH BECAUSE THEY ARE
TAUGHT NOT TO LIVE FULLY, AND SO KNOW THAT THEY
WILL DIE BEFORE THEY LIVE.

PEOPLE AREN'T HAPPY THAT THEY HAD A CHANCE TO LIVE
BECAUSE, AS I SAID, PEOPLE DON'T GET A CHANCE TO
REALLY *LIVE*: THEY WORK AND SAVE TO PAY FOR THEIR
DEATH.

GALISTEO NEWS, SANTA FE, N.M.

HOW SMART CAN YOU GET?

AS SMART AS YOU WANT TO GET,

AS SMART AS YOU ARE WILLING TO WORK TO GET,

AS SMART AS THE PEOPLE YOU HANG OUT WITH,

AS SMART AS THE BOOKS YOU READ,

THE MOVIES AND TV YOU WATCH.

YOU CAN GET AS SMART AS "GOD,"

FOR GOD DWELLS WITHIN YOU.

■

GALISTEO NEWS, SANTA FE, N.M.

WHICH TEACHES A PERSON MORE: PAIN OR HAPPINESS?

AN INQUIRING MIND. WITHOUT IT, NEITHER PAIN NOR HAPPINESS "TEACHES."

■

HUDSON STREET PAPERS, N.Y.C.

IF THE LIGHT WITHIN IS DARKNESS, HOW GREAT THEN IS THE DARKNESS WHEN THE LIGHT IS PUT OUT?

VAST AND DEEP ENOUGH TO DIVE INTO, GREAT ENOUGH TO PENETRATE, SO SIMILAR TO THE ESSENTIAL ENVIRON-MENT OF SOUL THAT IT BECOMES LIGHT ONCE IT'S IMMERSED IN.

THE GAMUT, SANTA FE, N.M.

MY FATHER DIED SIX MONTHS AGO. HOW MAY I EXPERIENCE THE OCCASIONAL SWEET GRIEF WITHOUT SUCCUMBING TO SADNESS?

REVIEW AND REFRESH YOUR CONCEPTS OF DEATH. GET TRANSCENDENTAL WITH IT; RELEASE THE WESTERN APPALLMENT WITH THIS MOST INEVITABLE OF EXPERI-ENCES. THINK OF DEATH AS A JOURNEY TO ANOTHER LAND. YOUR SADNESS IS ONLY YOUR OWN ATTACHMENT.

■

GALISTEO NEWS, SANTA FE, N.M.

HOW DO I FIND TRUST?

RELY ON THE STRENGTH OF NAKEDNESS.

■

THE VILLAGE VOICE, N.Y.C.

WHY DID ROBERTO CLEMENTE DIE?

ROBERTO CLEMENTE, THE ACE RIGHT FIELDER OF ALL TIME IN SOME SPORTS BUFFS' OPINION, WAS KILLED IN A PLANE CRASH (IN 1972, I BELIEVE) WHILE TRAVELING ON A GOODWILL MISSION TO NICARAGUA. WHY, YOU ASK? BECAUSE HE WAS SUCH A FINE SOUL, HE DESERVED TO BE TAKEN OFF THIS WEARYING MORTAL COIL. HE HAD, AFTER ALL, ACHIEVED A GREAT MEASURE OF PERSONAL SUCCESS; MAYBE, THEN, HE HAD ACTUALLY ACCOMPLISHED HIS SOUL'S REASON FOR COMING TO BIRTH AND WAS READY TO TAKE PART IN THE LIFE OF SUBTLER PLANES.

THE GAMUT, SANTA FE, N.M.

WHAT ARE TEARS?

TEARS ARE THE LUBRICANTS THAT EASE THE FLOW OF

PAIN.

■

THE GAMUT, SANTA FE, N.M.

WHAT SHOULD YOU DO WHEN CAUGHT
BETWEEN A ROCK AND A HARD PLACE?

LIE DOWN AND BASK IN THE SUN. LEAN BACK AND READ

IN THE SHADE. SIT UP AND MEDITATE. STAND UP AND

SCREAM.

■

GALISTEO NEWS, SANTA FE, N.M.

I HAVE AIDS. I WANT TO KNOW HOW YOU
FIND INNER PEACE BEFORE DEATH.

I HAVE THOUGHT ABOUT THIS ALL MY LIFE: HOW TO FACE

DEATH WITHOUT FEAR, WITHOUT HOLDING ON TO THE

LIFE THAT MUST BE LET GO OF. BUT THINK AS I MIGHT, I AM

NOT AT THE THRESHOLD, AS YOU ARE, SO THOUGH YOU

ASK ME, YOU ARE CLOSER TO THE ANSWER THAN I AM.

HOWEVER, WERE I IN YOUR SITUATION, I THINK I WOULD

SEEK CENTERING OF MYSELF INTO CONNECTION WITH

THE LESS DENSE REALMS OF REALITY: MEDITATE, CONTEM-

PLATE THESE ETHERIC FEELING-PLACES OF "SPIRIT." I

THINK, TOO, I WOULD USE MY REMAINING TIME TO

ACCOMPLISH THE FINER TASKS I'VE ASPIRED TO, TO MAKE PEACE WITH STILL RAW RELATIONSHIPS. BASICALLY, I THINK I WOULD PRACTICE FEELING LOVE FOR AS MUCH OF LIFE AS POSSIBLE.

■

THE GAMUT, SANTA FE, N.M.

WHAT IS THE HUMAN SITUATION—IN AN EXPLAINED WORD?

TRANSFORMATION. WE MUST GO THROUGH AND THROUGH, ACROSS, OVER, AND BEYOND THE ANIMAL APPEARANCE AND FORM WE'VE SCOURGED THE PLANET AND OURSELVES WITH THROUGHOUT EARTH TIME; MUST MUTATE NOW AND AVOID THE MAD RUSH OF HOLO-CAUSTAL NECESSITY. THIS HAS ALWAYS BEEN THE HUMAN SITUATION, BUT NOW IT IS THE HUMAN IMPERATIVE.

■

GALISTEO NEWS, SANTA FE, N.M.

HOW DOES ONE BECOME A PERSON OF CHARACTER?

ONE KEEPS ON TRUCKIN' ONE'S DREAMS, GOALS, IDEAS, AND INDIVIDUALITY ACROSS THE HIGHWAYS, FIXING UP THE WRECKS AND FLATS THAT ARE SURE TO OCCUR, PER-SEVERING THROUGH BLIZZARDS, IDIOTS, WARS, AND LOVE AFFAIRS, UNTIL THE COURSE IS RUN.

SHAKESPEARE & CO., N.Y.C.

WHAT IS THE SYMBOLIC SIGNIFICANCE
OF A COCKROACH?

TRANSMUTATION. LIKE THE HARD-SHELLED SCARAB OF ANCIENT EGYPT, THE COCKROACH IS A CREATURE THAT RISES FROM THE DEPTHS OF POLLUTION, BRINGING ITS LIFE FORCE INTO TRIUMPHANT VICTORY REGARDLESS OF CIRCUMSTANCES. THE SCARAB OF YORE CARRIED ITSELF OUT OF THE MUCK AND MIRE OF BLIND-WATER EMOTION-ALISM; THE COCKROACH CARRIES ITSELF OUT OF DDT DEATH, CONTINUING THE SPECIES THROUGH GENETIC TRANSMUTATION. THE COCKROACH WE SQUASH IS HERE TO TEACH US HOW TO CHANGE POISON INTO LIFE'S ELIXIR. FITTING THAT NEW YORK, CITY OF SHIVA THE DESTROYER, HAS SO MANY OF THE LITTLE TEACHERS!

THE GAMUT, SANTA FE, N.M.

DEAR ONE OF GOOD UNDERSTANDING, KNOWLEDGE, KIND HEART, AND UNLIMITED SOUL: I HAVE EVERYTHING IN LIFE RIGHT NOW. I HAVE LOVE, MONEY, FRIENDS, FAMILY, A JOB, ETC. HOW DO I GET ONE THING BACK: MY CURIOSITY AND MYSTERY OF LIFE? I DON'T FEEL ALL TOGETHER, YET I HAVE EVERYTHING. I NEED SOMETHING!
—"Age 18 Going on 400"

DEAR ANCIENT SOUL BORED WITH EASE:

THE WISDOM OF INSECURITY IS THAT INSECURITY PROVOKES CURIOSITY AND LIVES IN MYSTERY. GIVE UP ALL YOUR GOODIES, MAKE ROOM FOR SOMETHING NEW TO ENTER. JOIN THE NOUVEAU GYPSIES, THE FREE-FLOW ON-THE-EDGERS. RISK LIVING TRUE TO YOUR HEART. DARE TO EARN MONEY ONLY THROUGH WORK THAT SUITS YOUR VISION AND TALENT, THAT HAS A HELPING PURPOSE IN THE WORLD. IMPROVISE. LISTEN TO YOUR INNER FLUTE AND LET IT DANCE YOU THROUGH LIFE: CURIOSITY AND MYSTERY WILL ALWAYS BE WITH YOU.

■

COLLEGE OF SANTA FE, SANTA FE, N.M.

WHAT'S THE POINT OF ASKING QUESTIONS IF WE'RE ALL GOING TO BE DEAD IN FORTY YEARS?

WHY WASTE FORTY *MORE* YEARS IN IGNORANCE?

THE VILLAGE VOICE, N.Y.C.

**I AM AN EIGHTEEN-YEAR-OLD IDEALOGUE IN
SEARCH OF TRUTHS. WILL I FIND ANY IN THE
COLLEGE I PLAN TO ATTEND?**

OF COURSE. TRUTHS ARE TO BE FOUND ANY- AND EVERY-
WHERE. THE MORE PENETRATING YOUR PERCEPTION, THE
MORE TRUTHS YOU WILL FIND. I VENTURE, THOUGH, THAT
YOU WILL FIND MORE TRUTHS IN THE EVERYDAY, EXPERI-
ENTIAL ASPECT OF COLLEGE THAN IN THE LESSONS BEING
TAUGHT.

COLLEGE OF SANTA FE, SANTA FE, N.M.

**WHAT IS THE SOUND OF ABSOLUTE SILENCE?
OR: WHAT DOES A DEAF PERSON HEAR?**

THE ROAR OF SURFING MOLECULES.

LOOKING GLASS BOOKSTORE, PORTLAND, ORE.

MAKE A STATEMENT REGARDING LIVING LIFE TO THE FULLEST, DIRECTED TO TEENAGERS.

QUESTION AUTHORITY. FIND WHO YOU ARE, HOW YOU ARE, AND WHAT THAT INCLINES YOU TO WORK AT AND OCCUPY YOUR LIFE PURSUING—AND DO THIS. REMEMBER THE RULE OF HARMLESSNESS IN YOUR DEALINGS WITH HUMANS AND OTHER LIVING CREATURES. KEEP IN MIND, TOO, THAT CHANGE EQUALS STABILITY IN THIS WORLD: AS THE SEASONS GO, SO DO THE RHYTHMS OF LIFE FLUX AND FLOW. BE RESILIENT. FIND A METHOD OF CENTERING AND USE IT DAILY AND WHEN YOU ARE THROWN OFF KILTER. LOVE EXPERIENCE; LET IT OPEN THE FLOWER OF YOUR MIND AND NATURE.

■

GALISTEO NEWS, SANTA FE, N.M.

WHAT IS THE GREATEST OF MANKIND'S FEARS?

DEATH: LITTLE ONES, LIKE CHANGE; AND THE BIG ONE.

■

GALISTEO NEWS, SANTA FE, N.M.

WHAT DO YOU MAKE OF CONVENTIONAL WISDOM WHEN YOU ARE UNCONVENTIONAL?

I STAY AWAY FROM CONVENTIONS.

GALISTEO NEWS, SANTA FE, N.M.

IN THIS DAY, AGE, AND PLACE, WHERE IT IS SO FASHIONABLE TO BE IN SEARCH OF SPIRITUAL AND EMOTIONAL WHOLENESS, HOW DOES ONE STAY IN TOUCH WITH THEIR INNER VOICE TOWARDS TRUTH WITHOUT HOPPING ON THE FIRST AVAILABLE BANDWAGON, FOLLOWING FOR BELONGING RATHER THAN STRIVING FOR ONENESS?

KEEP LISTENING TO YOUR RESPONSE TO THE BANDWAGONS YOU FIND ATTRACTIVE ENOUGH TO JUMP ON. THEY'LL TAKE YOU SOMEWHERE, THESE WAGONS, BUT THE PLACE THEY'RE REALLY MEANT TO TAKE YOU TO IS YOUR OWN BANDWAGON. KEEP QUESTIONING YOUR REASONS FOR TRAVELING THE SPIRITUAL ROUTES.

■

GALISTEO NEWS, SANTA FE, N.M.

WHAT ASPECT OR ELEMENT OF LIFE MAKES PEOPLE TRULY HAPPY?

NATURE'S HEALING, EXHILARATING, INSPIRING BEAUTY.

GALISTEO NEWS, SANTA FE, N.M.

WHY IS WHY THE BASIC QUESTION OF LIFE?

BECAUSE

LIFE OFTEN SEEMS SO POINTLESS

SO CONFUSING

SO CONTRADICTORY

SO PAINFUL

SO HARD

SO "ONLY ONE LEG TO STAND ON."

WE FOCUS OUR FRUSTRATION IN THE SLING OF THE Y,

HOPING TO HIT THE POINT THAT SHIFTS OUR VIEW.

■

THE GAMUT, SANTA FE, N.M.

WHAT DOES LIGHT MEAN TO YOU—ITS IMPORTANCE IN ONE'S ENVIRONMENT?

LIGHT BRINGS SIGHT.

LIGHT BRINGS CLARITY.

LIGHT BRINGS JOY.

BUT LIGHT CAN ALSO POINT OUT THE FLAWS, THE CRACKS, THE CREVICES AND FAULT LINES IN PEELING-PAINT WALLS. IN THIS WAY, LIGHT IS A CATALYST FOR CHANGE, TRANSFORMATION, REBIRTH. LIGHT DELIGHTS AND HEALS MIND, BODY, AND SOUL WITH COLOR. LIGHT MAKES THIS REALITY POSSIBLE, AND RAINBOWS TOO.

ZIA DINER, SANTA FE, N.M.

WHAT DOES BEAUTY POSSESS?

THE VIEWER.

■

GALISTEO NEWS, SANTA FE, N.M.

MY FRIENDS AT ST. JOHN'S COLLEGE AND I HAVE BEEN CONTEMPLATING THIS QUESTION FOR A LONG TIME NOW: IS THE SOUL PREDICATE TO THE SENSES, OR ARE THE SENSES PREDICATE TO THE SOUL?
—"Bewildered New Yorker"

THE SENSES ARE BASED ON THE SOUL, IN THAT THE SOUL, AS THE ESSENCE OF A PERSON, EXISTS FIRST. HOWEVER, THE SOUL LEARNS THROUGH THE SENSES, MAKING THE SENSES AN INDISPENSABLE ADJUNCT TO THE SOUL'S LIFE. THE SENSES ARE PART OF THE PACKAGE OF PHYSICAL BODY. THE SOUL EXISTS WITHOUT THE PHYSICAL BODY, NOT ONLY ACCORDING TO THEOLOGIES BUT ALSO ACCORDING TO *AMERICAN HERITAGE DICTIONARY*, WHICH DEFINES SOULS AS "FORMING AN IMMATERIAL ENTITY DISTINGUISHED FROM BUT TEMPORALLY COEXISTENT WITH THE BODY."

ZIA DINER, SANTA FE, N.M.

**THE SELF
IN TRUTH
WOULD BE
FREE IN
ANY TIME
SPACE.**

TRUE

TRUTH SETS YOU FREE

BUT THE SELF

EVEN IN TRUTH

IS BOUND IN PATTERN

OR IT WOULD NOT BE SELF

IT WOULD BE

THE

TRUTH.

■

GALISTEO NEWS, SANTA FE, N.M.

I'M A GEMINI. TELL ME ABOUT MYSELF.

YOU'RE CHANGEABLE, MENTAL, LIKE TO YAK-YAK, MIX WITH PEOPLE, FLIRT, AND FLY TO PARTIES AND OTHER SOCIAL EVENTS. YOU ARE MOST INTERESTED IN BEING WITH PEOPLE, COMMUNICATING, CIRCULATING IDEAS. YOU FLIT FROM INFORMATION TO INFORMATION, TENDING TO GATHER AND DISSEMINATE RATHER THAN DEEPLY INVESTIGATE WHAT YOU FIND OUT. YOU MAKE AN INTERESTING

REPORTER, THEREFORE, BUT SUFFER THE SAME CRITICISM FOR LACK OF DEPTH AND THOROUGHNESS THAT THE MEDIA MENTORS DO.

■

SHAKESPEARE & CO., N.Y.C.

THE AGE-OLD QUESTION: IF A TREE FALLS IN THE WOODS AND NOBODY IS THERE TO HEAR IT, DOES IT MAKE ANY SOUND?

IT SOUNDS FOR "GOD," FOR WHOM ALL THINGS ARE PURE SOUND. WHEN YOU SAY "NOBODY," DO YOU INCLUDE ANIMALS, WORMS, BUTTERFLIES, BEETLES, ROCKS, LICHEN, BIRDS? FOR *THEM*, THE FALLING TREE MAKES A SOUND. IF YOU ARE NOT AWARE OF AN ARGUMENT TRANSPIRING IN CHINA, DOES THIS MEAN IT IS NOT HAPPENING?

■

STAGHORN, N.Y.C.

HOW DO YOU CREATE BELIEF IN THE UNBELIEVING?

ONLY ONE'S OWN EXPERIENCE CAN CREATE BELIEF, I.E., *SEEING* IS BELIEVING. YOU CAN CREATE *INTEREST* IN SOME-ONE ELSE'S MIND, BUT THE CERTAINTY OF BELIEF COMES ONLY WITH PERSONAL PROOF. ALWAYS I'VE FELT THAT THERE WAS A CONTINUANCE OF LIFE AFTER PHYSICAL DEATH, BUT MY INTELLECTUAL REALMS WERE NEVER ABLE

TO EMBRACE THIS THEORY TOTALLY. THEN MY LOVER DIED, AND I EXPERIENCED HIS PRESENCE AFTERWARD; NOT FOR A MOMENT, BUT FOR MONTHS THEREAFTER. I FELT HIM LEAVE A SECOND TIME, AS IF THE SOUL WERE NOW MOVING ON, AS THE BODY HAD BEFORE. THIS EXPERIENCE OVERRODE ALL MY INTELLECTUAL ARGUMENTS AND MADE A "BELIEVER" OF ME. EVEN IN ANSWERING THESE QUESTIONS, I CONSIDER MY *EXPERIENCE* TO BE THE ONLY VALID SOURCE FOR MY ANSWERS; THEORY IS SO MUCH AIR, WITHOUT THE PUDDING AS PROOF. THE TRUE METAPHYSICIAN IS A SCIENTIST, IN THAT ALL THEORIES ARE TESTED IN THE INNER LABORATORY. THAT'S THE ONLY WAY TO CREATE TRUE BELIEVING, WHICH THEN IS *KNOWING*.

■

GALISTEO NEWS, SANTA FE, N.M.

WHAT IS THE PURPOSE OF LIFE?

EXPERIENCE. LIFE IS A VERBAL EVENT, ALWAYS THRUSTING TOWARD INTERACTION, PROCESS, AND *MORE*.

■

HUDSON STREET PAPERS, N.Y.C.

WHY ME?

YOU'RE THE MOST LIKELY CANDIDATE, OBVIOUSLY: YOU WERE IN THE LINE OF FIRE!

GALISTEO NEWS, SANTA FE, N.M.

HOW DOES THINKING BECOME CREATIVE OR DESTRUCTIVE?

BY DISCONNECTING THOUGHT FROM HEART, THINKING BECOMES DESTRUCTIVE. BY REFERRING THOUGHT TO HEART CENTER, THINKING BECOMES CREATIVE.

THE VILLAGE VOICE, N.Y.C.

WHAT IS YOUR CONCEPT OF GOD?

PURE ENERGY.

GALISTEO NEWS, SANTA FE, N.M.

WHAT ARE EMOTIONS? I WANNA KNOW!

EMOTIONS ARE THE MOVEMENT OUT OF HIDING OF ONE'S INNER REACTIONS TO CURRENT PERSONAL EVENTS. *AMERICAN HERITAGE DICTIONARY* SAYS THAT EMOTIONS ARE THE "AGITATION OF THE PASSIONS OR SENSIBILITIES OFTEN INVOLVING PHYSIOLOGICAL CHANGES." THE ROOT OF THE WORD IS *EMOVERE,* TO MOVE OUT, STIR UP, EXCITE: *EX =* OUT, *MOVERE =* TO MOVE.

GALISTEO NEWS, SANTA FE, N.M.

WHERE IS THE NECTAR OF MY LIFE, AND WHERE MIGHT I SIP IT?

THE NECTAR IS ALL AROUND YOU AND WITHIN YOU. YOU MAY SIP IT BEST IN THE TEMPLE YOU CREATE TO CONNECT WITH THE ALL. THIS IS WHAT SACRED SPACES ARE FOR. ALL SPACE IS SACRED, BUT FOR TUNING TO THE NECTAR, A SPECIAL PLACE IS OPTIMUM.

■

GALISTEO NEWS, SANTA FE, N.M.

WHY IS LIFE SUCH A BITCH?

AS YOU KNOW, "GOD" SPELLED BACKWARD IS "DOG"; AND AS YOU ALSO HAVE BEEN TOLD, EVERYTHING ON THIS EARTH IS BACKWARD RELATIVE TO THE TRUTH OF LIFE. THEREFORE, LIFE, THE MOTHER OF US ALL, BECAME MOST ENRAGED WHEN HUMANS, HER FAVORITE CHILDREN, BEGAN TO HONOR THE VAPOR OF "GOD" RATHER THAN THE SUBSTANCE OF HER CREATION, "DOG" ET AL. THIS TURNED LIFE INTO THE RAGGY BITCH SHE IS TODAY. NOW GO OUT AND BOW (AS IN DOWN, NOT WOW) TO THE NEXT DOG OR CAT OR MOUSE OR RAT OR THIEF OR COP YOU SEE, AND HELP MA REMEMBER HER LOVING SOFTNESS.

GALISTEO NEWS, SANTA FE, N.M.

WHY ARE WE "HERE" RATHER THAN SOMEPLACE ELSE?

—"Wanderer"

OH, WANDERER, YOU *ARE* SOMEPLACE ELSE! AT EVERY MOMENT, YOU'RE SOMEPLACE ELSE IN SPACE, AS THE WORLD TURNS, THE WIND BLOWS, THE MOLECULES MOVE, THE VIBRATIONS RIPPLE, THE MORPHIC FIELDS FLOW AROUND AND WITHIN YOU.

THE GAMUT, SANTA FE, N.M.

WHY DO PEOPLE RESENT THEIR SAVIORS?

BECAUSE THERE ARE NO SAVIORS, EXCEPT FOR THE SELF WITHIN, WHICH SOMETIMES IS AWAKENED BY THOSE WE CALL "SAVIORS." THOSE WE RELY ON TO OPEN THE PATH-WAY TO THE KINGDOM WITHIN NEVER CALL THEMSELVES "SAVIORS," AND IF THEY DO, THEY ARE TO BE SUSPECTED. ALL THOSE WHOSE WORK IS SPIRIT-OPENING KNOW "SAV-ING" IS AN INTERNAL PROCESS, BUT WE SHEEP-EMULATING HUMANS USUALLY PREFER TO GIVE THE SAVING POWER OVER TO SOMEONE/THING OTHER THAN OURSELVES.

THE VILLAGE VOICE, N.Y.C.

WHY WERE WE CREATED?

TO EXPLORE ALL POSSIBILITIES. ARE YOU
SUCCEEDING IN THIS?

■

STAGHORN, N.Y.C.

CAN YOUR MIND'S EYE SEE AS MUCH AS YOUR REAL ONE?

YOUR MIND'S EYE CAN SEE MANY WORLDS, MANY UNI-
VERSES, CAN SEE THE HIDDEN MEANINGS, THE INNER
THOUGHTS. COMPARED TO THE MIND'S EYE, THE "REAL"
EYE IS BLIND.

■

GALISTEO NEWS, SANTA FE, N.M.

IS LIFE REALLY A RIVER?

YES, AND RIGHT NOW WE'RE CAUGHT IN THE RAPIDS AND
ARE ABOUT TO HIT THE TOP OF THE WATERFALL!

LOOKING GLASS BOOKSTORE, PORTLAND, ORE.

WHAT IS THE MEANING OF LIFE?

WHATEVER YOU THINK IT TO BE.

I THINK THE MEANING OF LIFE IS *EXPERIENCE*.

AMERICAN HERITAGE DICTIONARY GIVES THE ETYMOLOGY THUSLY: THE ROOT OF THE WORD "LIFE" IS *LEIP*, "TO STICK, ADHERE; FAT." SO EXPERIENCE FITS HERE, IN THAT LIFE IS TO BE STUCK TO, IMMERSED IN, IMBIBED.

■

ZIA DINER, SANTA FE, N.M.

HOW CAN I TRUST LIFE AS IT IS FOR ME NOW?

BY TRUSTING *YOU* AS YOU ARE NOW.

EVEN IF YOU'RE NOT LIVING TRUE TO YOUR VOICE BECAUSE YOU HAVEN'T LEARNED TO HEAR IT,

TRUST YOU AS YOU ARE NOW, FOR SILENTLY, UNCONSCIOUSLY, YOU BROUGHT YOURSELF TO THIS QUESTION. THE QUESTION IS THE FIRST PART OF THE ANSWER. NOW YOU CAN LISTEN MORE CLOSELY TO THE *YOU* VOICE AND LET IT GUIDE YOU TO THE FULL ANSWER. THIS RISKY PATH OF PROCESS IS THE ONLY WAY TO BECOME AN EXPERT AT SURFING THE TIDES OF EXISTENCE.

GALISTEO NEWS, SANTA FE, N.M.

ESSENCE VS. PERSONALITY.

BEHIND THE HUSK OF PERSONALITY,

BEHIND THE HEART THAT PUMPS THE LIFEBLOOD,

BEHIND THE MIND THAT TIMES THE HEART,

BEHIND THE DNA THAT DESIGNED HUSK, HEART, MIND,

BEHIND THE QUARKS, MOLECULES, AND VIBRATORY

PATTERNS:

ESSENCE.

IT TAKES AS LONG FOR ESSENCE TO SHINE

THROUGH PERSONALITY

AS IT TAKES PERSONALITY TO BUILD

AROUND ESSENCE;

OR

IF NOT TIME, THEN HEAT

AS IN FURNACE MOLTEN CORE

HEAT

THAT MELTS

PERSONALITY

INTO

ESSENCE.

GALISTEO NEWS, SANTA FE, N.M.

WHAT'S THE DIFFERENCE BETWEEN LIGHT AND WATER?

DEPTH.

■

ZIA DINER, SANTA FE, N.M.

I AM HERE FOR THE ART AND THE SACRED CONFERENCE. OUR GROUP QUESTION IS, OF COURSE: WHAT IS SACRED?

EVERYTHING IS SACRED. NOTHING IS SACRED. OR, NOTH-ING IS MORE SACRED THAN ANYTHING ELSE. WHERE IS "GOD" NOT?

■

GALISTEO NEWS, SANTA FE, N.M.

I HAVE A TEACHER WHO TAUGHT ME ABOUT REALITY, BUT I WANT TO SPEND LESS TIME WITH HIM. HOW DO I KNOW IF I AM RESISTING THE TEACHING OR FINDING MY OWN WAY TO GOD?

WELL, *ARE* YOUR REALITY LESSONS DONE?
GURDJIEFF DEMANDED OF HIS BEST, TEN-YEAR STUDENT THAT SHE LEAVE HER NEW HUSBAND AND ACCOMPANY HIM, GURDJIEFF, ON A YEAR-LONG JOURNEY. SHE SAID TO HIM, "WHY DO YOU ASK ME TO DO THIS, THE ONE THING THAT YOU *KNOW* I CANNOT DO?" BUT GURDJIEFF MERELY SAID, "IF YOU DO NOT COME WITH ME, YOU WILL NEVER

SEE ME AGAIN." ON THE DEPARTURE MORNING, SHE WENT TO THE TRAIN STATION TO SEE HIM OFF. THEY EXCHANGED LOOKS, AND IN THAT LOOK WAS COMMUNICATED HER REFUSAL TO GO WITH HIM AND HIS GOODBYE FOREVER TO HER. INDEED, SHE NEVER SAW HIM AGAIN. SHE HAD LEARNED HER REALITY LESSON, THOUGH IT TOOK HER MANY YEARS TO UNDERSTAND THE RIGHTNESS OF HER ACTION AND THE WILINESS OF GURDJIEFF'S RELEASE-OF-DISCIPLE METHOD.

WHOSE WAY *WILL* YOU FOLLOW?

INTERNATIONAL WOMEN'S FORUM, SANTA FE, N.M.

HOW CAN WE FIND THE TIME TO EXPLORE ALL OUR SELVES—FROM APHRODITE TO HERA? HELP!

EXPLORE WHILE YOU EXPRESS IN YOUR DAILY ROUTINE. DEVELOP THE OBSERVER IN YOU—IS THERE A FEMININE ARCHETYPE FOR THE OBSERVER? ARTEMIS? THE HIGH PRIESTESS? WHATEVER YOU NAME IT, THE OBSERVER IN YOU NEEDS TO BE ACTIVE WHILE YOU ARE; THIS OBSERVER WILL OBSERVE THAT YOU RUN THROUGH *ALL* YOUR SELVES, FROM HERA TO APHRODITE, IN THE COURSE OF YOUR DAY. IT IS, AFTER ALL, OUR HUMAN BEHAVIOR THAT IS THE FOUNDATION OF THESE ARCHETYPES.

GALISTEO NEWS, SANTA FE, N.M.

WHY DO SOULS ADVANCE AT
DIFFERENT RATES?

BECAUSE DIFFERENT MOLECULES TRAVEL AT VARIED SPEEDS, OWING TO THE SHAPE THEY'RE IN AND THE FREQUENCY THEY'RE ENMESHED IN. DIFFERENCE IS AS CONSTANT IN CREATION AS CHANGE.

■

GALISTEO NEWS, SANTA FE, N.M.

HOW DO YOU TELL THE DIFFERENCE
BETWEEN THE FAKE AND THE REAL THING?

YOU TEST IT AGAINST YOUR OWN SENSE OF REALNESS.

■

GALISTEO NEWS, SANTA FE, N.M.

WHAT DOES "TO THINE OWN SELF BE TRUE"
MEAN TO YOU?

IT MEANS LIVING ME, AS I KNOW ME TO BE.

GALISTEO NEWS, SANTA FE, N.M.

**THE TERM "MORPHIC FIELDS" OCCURS WITH
HIGH FREQUENCY IN YOUR WRITINGS.
WHAT ARE MORPHIC FIELDS?
PLEASE EXPLAIN IN EARTHY TERMS.
—Sincerely, a fugitive from the New Age**

DEAR FUGITIVE:

MORPHIC FIELDS ARE AKIN TO THE ETHERIC BODY, OR THE
AURIC FIELD, THAT SURROUNDS EACH AND EVERY THING.
THE TERM WAS DEVELOPED BY THE CONTROVERSIAL
BRITISH BIOLOGIST RUPERT SHELDRAKE. MORE CAN BE
READ ABOUT MORPHIC FIELDS IN HIS BOOK *PRESENCE OF
THE PAST.* IN ESSENCE, SHELDRAKE POSITS THAT WITHIN
THESE MORPHIC FIELDS IS CONTAINED THE MEMORY FOR
DEVELOPMENT, OR, AS HE CALLS IT, THE "HABIT PATTERN"
THAT CREATES EACH AND EVERY THING; RATHER THAN
THE GENES AND DNA HOLDING THE TOTAL PATTERN OF
LIFE FORMS, THESE MORPHIC FIELDS CREATE US IN THE
MOLD OF OUR ANCESTORS.

■

STAGHORN, N.Y.C.

IS IT EVER TOO LATE?

OF COURSE!

SHAKESPEARE & CO., N.Y.C.

**SOMEONE ONCE MADE A REMARK TO THE
EFFECT THAT IT'S RELATIVELY EASY TO GET
"A"'S IN SCHOOL, BUT MUCH MORE
DIFFICULT TO GET AN "A" IN LIFE. WHAT
ARE THE "TEACHERS" AND "CLASSROOMS"
THAT TEACH US LIFE AND WHAT SHOULD WE
DO TO GET AN "A" IN THIS COURSE?**

WHAT IS *NOT* A TEACHER IN LIFE? BUT THE GREATEST TEACHERS ARE OUR LOVERS. WE LEARN MORE IN INTIMATE RELATIONSHIPS THAN IN ANY OTHER SPHERE OF EXPERIENCE. NEXT TO LOVERS, THE GREATEST TEACHERS ARE FOUND IN THE CLASSROOMS OF HARDSHIP. THE WAY TO GET AN "A" IN THE SCHOOL OF LIFE IS TO BEGIN WITH THE "A" OF AWARENESS. AFTER AWARENESS IS WAKENED, GROWTH BEGINS. WHEN GROWTH HAS PROGRESSED, THE "A" IS GIVEN FOR LIVING BY THE GOLDEN RULE—NOW TARNISHED INTO OBSCURITY—"DO UNTO OTHERS AS YOU WOULD HAVE THEM DO UNTO YOU." WHEN THIS LEVEL OF THE "A" GRADE HAS BECOME AN INTRINSIC PART OF ONE'S LIFE, THE "A" IS THEN EARNED FOR LEARNING NONATTACHMENT, WITH ITS ATTENDANT GRACE OF FULLY FEELING LOVE FOR ALL THAT IS.

LOOKING GLASS BOOKSTORE, PORTLAND, ORE.

WHY IS THE WORLD ROUND?

SO THE GODS CAN PLAY BALL.

■

THE GAMUT, SANTA FE, N.M.

DOES GOD CARE?

WHEN YOU CARE, GOD CARES.

■

STAGHORN, N.Y.C.

HOW DOES ONE END PART ONE AND START PART TWO IN THE MIDST OF A CRISIS?

ALONE.

■

GALISTEO NEWS, SANTA FE, N.M.

FREE WILL: SHIT? OR BULLSHIT?

POTENT BULLSHIT. THE CARROT OF FREE WILL IS HIGHLY FERTILIZING TO ACTION AND EXPERIENCE, AND EVENTUALLY TO UNDERSTANDING THAT ALL POSSIBILITIES FREE WILL CAN MANIFEST WERE WOVEN INTO THE ORIGINAL GRID OF CREATION. THE GAME IS STACKED IN FAVOR OF THE PATTERN.

THE VILLAGE VOICE, N.Y.C.

**IN SIX MILLION A.D., OUR HUMAN RACE IS
SCHEDULED FOR NATURAL EXTINCTION AND
ALSO FACES THE EMERGENCE OF TWO
HUMANOID STOCKS: HUMUNTIS AND
GALLICIANS.**

GOD, THERE'S SO MUCH WISDOM IN THE WORLD!

LOVE

HUDSON STREET PAPERS, N.Y.C.

WHO SAID
"LOVE IS THE ANSWER"?

EVERYONE.

WHAT DO WOMEN WANT FROM MEN?

GUIDE DANCE

LOVE

ADORATION

TO BE CHERISHED

TO BE MADE LOVE TO LONG AND TENDERLY AND

THOROUGHLY

TO ADORE

TO SURROUND

TO CARE FOR THEIR MAN.

AND THEY WANT THE FREEDOM TO DO ALL THIS OF

THEIR OWN VOLITION, NOT BECAUSE IT IS EXPECTED/

DEMANDED. THEY ALSO WANT FOREVER AND

MONOGAMY.

■

WHY IS LOVE MORE DIFFICULT THAN HATE?

LOVE REQUIRES ACCEPTANCE OF DIFFERENCES. HATRED
DESIRES TO DESTROY THEM. WE'RE MORE PRACTICED, WE
HUMANS, IN DESTRUCTION THAN IN ACCEPTANCE.

GALISTEO NEWS, SANTA FE, N.M.

WHAT DO MEN REALLY WANT FROM WOMEN?

A MIRROR OF THEIR BEST, STRONGEST SELF

FREEDOM

ENCOURAGEMENT

FREEDOM

CREATIVE, LUSTFUL SEX

FREEDOM

HELP IN GROWING, INNER AND OUTER

FREEDOM

FOOD

FREEDOM

LAUNDRY DONE, BEDS MADE

FREEDOM

SOMEONE TO PARADE AND WIN THE BEAUTY PRIZE

FREEDOM.

■

GALISTEO NEWS, SANTA FE, N.M.

WHAT DOES THE ARROW SAY TO THE HEART AS IT FLIES THROUGH THE AIR, READY TO PIERCE IT IN TRUE LOVE?

"ASSIMILATE *THIS!*"

THE GAMUT, SANTA FE, N.M.

AT THE RISK OF SOUNDING BRASH, I WOULD LIKE TO KNOW HOW TO MAKE WOMEN BECOME OVERWHELMED BY DESIRE AND ANIMAL LUST WITH JUST A LOOK OR AT MOST A CASUAL CONVERSATION.

FORGET IT, SWEETS—WOMEN DON'T GET "OVERWHELMED BY DESIRE & LUST" WITH JUST A LOOK OR *CASUAL* CONVERSATION! THAT'S A MAN'S GAME. WOMEN GET TURNED ON BY LONG AND DEEP CONVERSATIONS ABOUT HOW YOU THINK, FEEL, AND HAVE LIVED: AND BY THE FACT THAT YOU ARE INTERESTED IN HEARING ABOUT *THEIR* EXPERIENCES.

■

CARDS & SUCH, FOREST HILLS, N.Y.

WHY IS IT THAT WHEN I GO OUT WITH A GUY ONCE, THEY JUST DROP ME? I DON'T THINK I'M THAT UGLY, AND MY PERSONALITY IS OUTGOING.

MAYBE YOUR PERSONALITY IS *TOO* OUTGOING. MAYBE YOU WANT LOVE SO MUCH IT FRIGHTENS MEN. MAYBE THE MEN YOU'RE CHOOSING ARE RAVING, MACHISMO IDIOTS WHO SIMPLY CAN'T APPRECIATE THE SENSITIVITY OF A FEELINGFUL WOMAN.

THE GAMUT, SANTA FE, N.M.

IS THERE LOVE AT FIRST SIGHT?

YES, BUT IS THERE LOVE AT *SECOND* SIGHT

IS THE PROBLEM!

■

GALISTEO NEWS, SANTA FE, N.M.

QUANTUM MECHANICS
LOVE
RELATIONSHIP
WHY?
I KNOW TWO (2) THINGS: THERE ARE NO ABSOLUTES. PARADOX IS TENABLE.

I SEE IT SIMILARLY: PARADOX IS A CONSTANT. THAT'S THE SECRET WE'VE KEPT FROM OURSELVES, AND THE KEEPING OF THIS SECRET IS WHY WE'RE INSANE AS A HUMANITY. THE QUANTUM MECHANICS OF THIS PARADOXICAL FIELD, LIFE, IS INTERACTION: PARADOX BREEDS CURIOSITY, CURIOSITY INSPIRES INTERACTION, INTERACTION BRINGS ATTRACTION, ATTRACTION IS NAMED LOVE, AND LOVE MAKES US WANT TO BOARD THE OTHER'S SHIP. "WHY" IS ANSWERABLE ONLY IN "HOW."

■

HUDSON STREET PAPERS, N.Y.C.

WHY DO FOOLS LOVE TO RUSH IN WHERE ANGELS FEAR TO TREAD?

FOOLS KNOW WHERE THE FUN IS.

HUDSON STREET PAPERS, N.Y.C.

IF LOVE IS THE ANSWER, WHAT'S THE QUESTION?

"WHO ARE YOU?"

■

HUDSON STREET PAPERS, N.Y.C.

DEAR LOVE ADVISER:

WHAT'S THE BEST FOOD TO GET TO YOUR LOVER'S HEART? I'VE GOT MY BURNERS LIT, WAITING FOR A RESPONSE.

THE BEST FOOD TO GET YOUR LOVER'S HEART ON YOU MUST BE OFFERED IN SMALL DOSES AT FIRST AND MUST KEEP THE MOUTH TASTY AND JUICY. CAVIAR COMES TO MIND, SERVED WITH A RICH ST. EMILION BORDEAUX (UNLESS YOU'RE A TRADITIONALIST, IN WHICH CASE SERVE THE BEST CHAMPAGNE WITHIN YOUR AFFORDABILITY); ONIONS MAY BE INCLUDED, IF YOU'RE BOTH OF THE STRONG, EARTHY VARIETY. OTHERWISE, THE JUICY PEARLS OF PROTEIN WILL QUENCH APPETITE AND HUNGER AND GIVE YOUR MALE LOVER STAMINA. WHEN THE MELDING IS SATED, RENEW YOUR STRENGTHS WITH A HEARTY MEAL.

THE GAMUT, SANTA FE, N.M.

IF LOVE IS LIKE JAZZ, HOW COME YOU CAN'T TURN IT ON LIKE A RADIO?

YOU CAN—YOU'VE JUST GOT TO PUSH

THE RIGHT BUTTON!

■

GALISTEO NEWS, SANTA FE, N.M.

WHAT IS LOVE REALLY?

LOVE IS A FIELD, A RADIO STATION WE ALL HOPE TO TUNE IN TO. LOVE IS CONNECTION. LOVE IS UNDERSTANDING. LOVE COMES IN MANY FLAVORS: LOVE FOR CHILD, LOVE FOR FRIEND, LOVE FOR SPAGHETTI, LOVE FOR CHRISTMAS, LOVE FOR BOY OR GIRLFRIEND, LOVE FOR HUSBAND . . . HOPE YOU GET TO TASTE THEM ALL THOROUGHLY.

■

GALISTEO NEWS, SANTA FE, N.M.

THE LILIES HAVE DIED, AND NOW A ROSE HAS BLOSSOMED IN THEIR PLACE, GIVING ME A NEW SENSE OF LOVE THAT I WANT TO SHARE. WHY WON'T HE ACCEPT?

YOUR ROSE IS TOO COVERED WITH SCHMALTZ: MEN

CAN'T HANDLE TOO MUCH GOO.

THE VILLAGE VOICE, N.Y.C.

HOW DO YOU KNOW WHEN TO GIVE UP ON A GIRL WHEN SHE KEEPS TURNING YOU DOWN IN A NICE WAY WHEN YOU ASK HER FOR A DATE?

BELIEVE HER WORDS, AND SAVE YOUR ENERGY.

HUDSON STREET PAPERS, N.Y.C.

OH, WRITER IN THE WINDOW, HOW DOES ONE KEEP FROM BECOMING TOO DEPENDENT ON YOUR LOVED ONE?

KEEP BUSY WITH THE CREATION OF YOUR OWN LIFE.

HUDSON STREET PAPERS, N.Y.C.

IF LOVE MAKES THE WORLD GO ROUND, WHAT DOES LUST DO?

LUST MAKES YOU SCREAM FOR MORE—

LIKE CHINESE FOOD.

THE GAMUT, SANTA FE, N.M.

GOOD LOVING IS . . .

HARD TO FIND;

SOMETHING WE RARELY GIVE, EVEN TO OURSELVES;

WHAT WE ALL DESIRE MORE THAN ANYTHING ELSE;

FULL APPRECIATION OF THE NATURE OF A PERSON, TRUE
MIRRORING OF THE BEST QUALITIES AND POTENTIAL OF A
BEING, UNDERSTANDING OF A PERSON'S FAULTS AND FIS-
SURES AND THE FACT THAT IT TAKES TIME, NOT NAGGING,
TO TRANSFORM AND HEAL SOMEONE;

THE PLEASURING OF THE LOVED ONE, THE ART OF FIND-
ING JOY IN GIVING, AS WELL AS IN RECEIVING;

CONTINUAL REMEMBRANCE OF THE LOVE, DEMONSTRATED
OFTEN—WITH A TOUCH, A SMALL GIFT, A FLOWER, A SPE-
CIAL DINNER, A WEEKEND AWAY IN THE COUNTRY;

GRACEFUL RESPECT IN DEALING WITH EVERYONE;

PICKING UP LITTER WHEN YOU SEE IT.

GOOD LOVING STARTS WITHIN YOURSELF.

■

GALISTEO NEWS, SANTA FE, N.M.

WHAT MAKES LOVE LAST?

INTEREST.

THE GAMUT, SANTA FE, N.M.

WHAT DO YOU THINK OF ELEVEN YEARS DIFFERENCE BETWEEN MAN/WOMAN, HE THE YOUNGER?

I THINK THAT IS A FORTUITOUS LIAISON FOR BOTH. WOMAN IS AT HER FULL SEXUAL BLOSSOM AFTER THIRTY, AND MAN AT HIS WHILE HE'S YOUNG. I THINK THAT YOUNG MEN NEED THE TEACHING OF OLDER WOMEN IN ORDER TO FILL THEMSELVES OUT EMOTIONALLY AND SEXUALLY. HOWEVER, FROM THE WOMAN'S POINT OF VIEW, THIS LIAISON IS DANGEROUS: YOUNG MEN GET ITCHY TO TRY THEIR NEWFOUND KNOWLEDGE ON SWEETER, YOUNGER CHICKIE-PIES, WHILE THE OLDER WOMAN IS AT THE POINT WHERE SHE IS READY FOR A FULL-FLEDGED LONG-TERM FOUNDATIONAL RELATIONSHIP. HIS ITCHY FEET ARE LIKELY TO BREAK HER WISE AND WEARY HEART. SHE MUST LEARN TO WU-WEI: KNOW THE TIME FOR HOLDING AND THE TIME FOR LETTING GO.

■

HUDSON STREET PAPERS, N.Y.C.

WHAT DEMANDS CAN LOVE MAKE?

LOVE CANNOT DEMAND; IT CAN ONLY RADIATE.

NEED DEMANDS. LOVE GIVES.

THE GAMUT, SANTA FE, N.M.

IS THERE ANY ROMANCE LEFT IN THE WORLD?

TOO MUCH, THERE IS, BUT IN THE WRONG PLACES. WE NEED LESS ROMANCE IN OUR LOVE LIFE AND MORE IN OUR APPROACH TO THE LIFE EXPERIENCE.

HUDSON STREET PAPERS, N.Y.C.

HOW CAN A MOTHER WHO LOVES AND NURTURES HER BABY ALL DAY STILL HAVE ENOUGH LEFT OVER FOR HER LOVER AT NIGHT?

IT'S AN AGE-OLD PROBLEM, M'DEAR. PERHAPS YOU NEED TO REFRESH YOURSELF BEFORE YOUR LOVER ARRIVES, WITH A HOT BUBBLE-BATH SOAK IN THE CANDLELIGHT, YOUR FAVORITE HEALING MUSIC PLAYING, SIPPING THE BEST EUPHORIC AVAILABLE. CREATE A BRIDGE BETWEEN THE TWO WORLDS, A BRIDGE WHERE YOU LOVE *YOU* FOR A BRIEF BUT POTENT HOUR.

VERY SPECIAL ARTS, ALBUQUERQUE, N.M.

SHOULD ONE LET THE HEAD OR THE HEART RULE?

SURELY IT'S TIME THAT THEY RULE IN HARMONIOUS INTERACTION. TOGETHER.

GALISTEO NEWS, SANTA FE, N.M.

WHAT IS TRUE LOVE?
(IT'S LIKE: ME AND CHERYL JUST WANTED
TO KNOW IF WE HAD IT OR NOT.)

TRUE LOVE PENETRATES TO THE CORE OF THE LOVED ONE; REMAINS VIBRANT IN THE FACE OF BOILS, TOILS, AND DENTURES.

("TRUE" = "CONSISTENT WITH FACT OR REALITY" —*AMERICAN HERITAGE DICTIONARY*)

■

THE GAMUT, SANTA FE, N.M.

OH, DEAR WRITER IN THE WINDOW: PLEASE
SPEAK TO US MORTALS ABOUT THE
IMMORTAL BULLET OF LOVE.

THE IMMORTAL BULLET OF LOVE SLAYS THE EGO, MELTS THE ARMOR, TAKES THE THORNS OUT OF INTELLECT, AND OPENS THE DOORS OF INTUITION. THE IMMORTAL BULLET OF LOVE IS SHOT FROM THE CANNON OF SPIRIT, NOT THE GUN OF LINGAM OR THE SLING OF YONI, AND IT AIMS AT THE SOULHEART. MAY YOU, DEAR READER, BE SHOT THROUGH, RIDDLED, WITH THE IMMORTAL BULLETS OF LOVE.

ZIA DINER, SANTA FE, N.M.

HOW CAN MEN EXPAND AND GROW AND BE TRUE TO THEMSELVES WITHOUT FEELING THEY NEED TO ATONE FOR PAST MALE CRIMES?

THEY CAN'T. MEN HAVE GOT TO RECOGNIZE THEIR GENETIC AT-ONE-MENT WITH "MALE CRIMES"; THEY MUST LOOK TESTOSTERONE IN THE EYE IN ORDER TO UNDERSTAND HOW TO USE AND NOT ABUSE IT, TO EXPAND IT IN A CARING, CONSTRUCTIVE DIRECTION.

■

ZIA DINER, SANTA FE, N.M.

IF SOMEONE DOES NOT LOVE THEMSELF, CAN THEY TRULY LOVE ANOTHER?

THEY DO THE BEST THEY CAN.

WHO AMONG US TRULY LOVES ONE'S SELF? WHO AMONG US TRULY LOVES ANOTHER? WE TAKE LOVE TOO SERIOUSLY AND GET VERY LITTLE OF IT FOR OUR EXERTION. I THINK LOVE IS THE FIELD OF EXISTENCE—YOU, ME, THE PAPER YOU'RE READING, THE WORDS YOU'RE HEARING. LOVE IS LIFE, AND THAT'S WHY LIFE IS SUCH A CODEPENDENT EXPERIENCE. LIFE, AT LEAST ON EARTH, IS A POLARITY FIELD, THE NEGATIVE ALWAYS ATTRACTING THE POSITIVE. IF YOU GRAVITATE TOWARD ME FOR WHATEVER REASON, YOU LOVE ME.

■

ZIA DINER, SANTA FE, N.M.

WHAT DO *YOU* KNOW ABOUT WHAT MEN NEED TO DO IN ORDER TO EXPAND AND GROW?! ENOUGH FEMINIST GUILT ALREADY!

I KNOW WHAT I'VE EXPERIENCED WITH MEN, AND FROM THOSE INTERACTIONS AND THEIR EFFECTS ON ME, I OFFER MY "CRITIQUE" AND SUGGESTIONS FOR CHANGE. YOU MISUNDERSTAND ME. THESE CRITIQUES ARE NOT GIVEN TO INSPIRE GUILT. GUILT IS THE RESPONSE OF PERSONS UNWILLING TO SELF-EXAMINE AND ANGRY AT BEING CON-FRONTED ABOUT THEIR ACTION; GUILT ORIGINATED WITH THE PARENTAL FINGER-WAGGING BAD-BOY ROUTINE. I MEAN TO INSPIRE INTROSPECTION. I MEAN TO POINT OUT TO YOU THAT THERE ARE DESTRUCTIVE PATTERNS TO BE LOOKED AT, SO THAT RELATIONSHIPS, WITH WORLD AND WOMAN, CAN BE NOURISHING AGAIN. I THINK WOMEN, TOO, HAVE NEGATIVE PATTERNS TO EXAMINE AND RESHAPE, BUT I THINK WOMEN ARE WORKING ON THESE

AND ARE MORE WILLING THAN MEN TO "KOP" AND CHANGE. I'M NOT SAYING YOU'RE WRONG, BAD, DEAD-IN-THE-WATER, FOR HAVING NEGATIVE PATTERNS WHEN IT COMES TO DEALING WITH WOMEN AND MAYBE WITH LIFE. I'M SAYING THAT WE ARE ALL VICTIMS OF SOCIETY'S AND OUR PARENTS' MISTAKEN, OBSOLETE, BUT MAYBE WELL-MEANING PHILOSOPHIES OF LIFE, AND WE HUMANS ALL CAN ONLY GAIN BY REEXAMINING THE CONDITIONING THAT OUR BEHAVIOR AS MEN AND WOMEN SPRINGS FROM.

■

GALISTEO NEWS, SANTA FE, N.M.

HOW WILL I LEARN TO TRUST YET ONE MORE MAN?

DON'T. LOOK INSTEAD AT YOUR HISTORY WITH MEN, FROM BOTH SIDES: THE KIND OF MALE YOU GRAVITATE TOWARD, THE GAMES HE TENDS TO PLAY; AND THE GAMES *YOU* PLAY, THE CONDITIONING *YOU* ARE UNABLE TO UNLOCK FROM. DEAL WITH WHAT YOU OBSERVE IN YOURSELF. DO YOU WANT TO CHANGE? IS IT WORTH THE EFFORT? DO YOU PERCEIVE FROM WHAT YOU'VE EXPERIENCED THUS FAR IN LIFE THAT YOU CAN MEET A MAN WHO IS WILLING AND ABLE TO UNLOCK THE CONDITIONING *HE* HAS BEEN ENCODED WITH? TRUST YOURSELF.

THE LIVING BATCH BOOKSTORE, ALBUQUERQUE, N.M.

WHY DO MOMS AND DADS FIGHT?
(Asked by a six-year-old boy)

BECAUSE TIME HAS CAUSED THEM TO FORGET THAT THEY LOVE EACH OTHER.

BECAUSE THEY MARRIED TOO YOUNG AND HAD NOT WORKED OUT THEIR KINKS AND THEIR NEED TO EXPERIENCE LIFE.

BECAUSE THEY ARE EMOTIONALLY PROBLEMED AND DO NOT HAVE RESOURCES, OR PERHAPS COURAGE, TO SEEK HELP IN UNDERSTANDING THEMSELVES AND THEIR FRUSTRATIONS.

■

THE GAMUT, SANTA FE, N.M.

IS MY MOM REALLY A BITCHY PERSON, OR DOES SHE JUST ACT THAT WAY?

SHE JUST ACTS THAT WAY, IN RESPONSE TO LIFE'S SNAGS AND PROBLEMS, AND THE BURDENS OF BRINGING UP CHILDREN AND HUSBANDS. SHE'S PROBABLY GOT SENSITIVE NERVES AND NEEDS A REST. TRY AND UNDERSTAND HER: BEING A MOM IS A BITCHINGLY DIFFICULT JOB!

STAGHORN, N.Y.C.

WHY DON'T PARENTS LEAVE THEIR KIDS ALONE TO LEAD THEIR OWN LIVES?
(Asked by a ten-year-old)

HOW MANY KIDS DO YOU KNOW WHO ARE READY TO GET A JOB, PAY THE RENT, PAY A PHONE BILL, COOK DINNERS, CROSS THE STREET, TAKE THE SUBWAY, ALL BY THEMSELVES? SO AS LONG AS YOU NEED TO BE TAUGHT THESE THINGS, AND HAVE THESE THINGS PROVIDED FOR YOU BY THE HARD WORK OF YOUR PARENTS, YOUR PARENTS CAN'T LEAVE YOU ALONE TO LEAD A LIFE YOU DON'T KNOW HOW TO LEAD; AND SINCE IT'S THEIR MONEY AND WORK, THEY HAVE THE RIGHT TO ASK YOU TO OBEY THEIR RULES. ENJOY THIS FREEDOM FROM RESPONSIBILITY WHILE YOU'VE GOT IT—YOU'LL NEVER HAVE IT AGAIN!

■

THE GAMUT, SANTA FE, N.M.

WHY ARE MY PARENTS ALWAYS MAD AT ME?

RAISING CHILDREN ISN'T EASY. ENDURING THE TRIBULATIONS OF A GROWING CHILD CAN DRIVE A PARENT UP THE PROVERBIAL WALL. SO BE PATIENT AND UNDERSTANDING WITH YOUR PARENTS. THEY WORK HARD TO GIVE YOU FOOD, SHELTER, AND ALL THE OTHER GOODIES YOU ASK THEM FOR.

LOOKING GLASS BOOKSTORE, PORTLAND, ORE.

DO YOU HAVE SOME WONDERFUL ADVICE TO NEW PARENTS IN THE NINETIES IN AMERICA?

TO PARAPHRASE CROSBY, STILLS, ET AL., TEACH YOUR CHILDREN WELL THE DREAMS YOU GREW ON. BRING THEM INTO EARLY KNOWLEDGE OF THE ETERNAL AS THE REAL. HELP THEM UNDERSTAND EARTH-LIFE IS FOR LEARNING, FOR EXPERIENCING, AND NOT FOR CLINGING TO. TEACH THEM THAT DEATH IS AN ASPECT OF LIFE; ELIMINATE THE FEAR OF IT. SHOW THEM IN YOUR RELATIONSHIP WHAT LOVING IS, THAT HARSH WORDS ARE TEMPORARY EXPLOSIONS THAT DO NOT ELIMINATE YOUR ABILITY TO CARE FOR EACH OTHER. REMEMBER THAT YOU ARE VEHICLES FOR THE NURTUREMENT AND GUIDE-DANCE OF THE SOUL WITHIN YOUR CHILD; YOU ARE NOT THE MAKERS OR SCRIPTWRITERS OF THEIR DESTINY. REMEMBER TO RESPECT YOUR CHILD'S IDEAS AS A VOICE OF THE FUTURE, RATHER THAN SEEING THEM AS A DEGRADATION OF YOUR OWN VALUES THAT YOU DESIRE TO IMPOSE UPON YOUR OFFSPRING. THIS LAST IS MOST IMPORTANT IN THE TEEN YEARS, WHEN YOUTH'S NOTIONS TAKE ON FULL COLTLIKE FERVOR, AND LACK OF UNDERSTANDING IN PARENTS SENDS TEENAGERS REBELLING. EVERY YEAR, REFRESH YOUR PARENTHOOD WITH A REREADING OF KAHLIL GIBRAN'S POEM ON CHILDREN IN *THE PROPHET*.

THE VILLAGE VOICE, N.Y.C.

WHERE IS HE?

HIDING FROM THE FURY OF FEMALE INDIGNATION.

■

HUDSON STREET PAPERS, N.Y.C.

WHERE IS SHE?

HIDING IN WORK WHILE SHE WAITS FOR YOU TO REALIZE
AND HONOR HER WISDOM.

■

HUDSON STREET PAPERS, N.Y.C.

WHAT'S THE DIFFERENCE BETWEEN
MEN AND WOMEN?

MEN ARE OUTWARD BOUND, WOMEN INWARD TURNED.

MEN HAVE MANY SEEDS TO SPREAD, WOMEN HAVE ONE
CAVERN TO GROW ONE SEED AT A TIME (SOMETIMES TWO,
RARELY FIVE).

MEN LIVE IN THE MOMENT OF ACTION. WOMEN LIVE IN
THE MIND OF RELATIONSHIPS. ASK A MAN IF HE THINKS
ABOUT HIS RELATIONSHIP CONTINUALLY. EIGHT TIMES
OUT OF TEN, HE WILL SAY "NO." ASK A WOMAN; NINE
TIMES OUT OF NINE, SHE'LL SAY "YES."

MEN'S EMOTIONS HAVE LAIN DORMANT FOR TOO LONG;
WOMEN'S INTELLECTS HAVE SLEPT, INACTIVE FOR TOO
LONG.

MEN FIGHT. WOMEN LOVE. WOMEN GIVE BIRTH, MEN GIVE DEATH. WOMEN KNOW HOW TO BE PARENTS. MEN HAVE LOST THE KNACK. MEN HAVE TO HAVE LOVE AND FREEDOM. WOMEN LONG TO HAVE LOVE AND SECURITY. NEITHER MEN NOR WOMEN WERE BROUGHT UP TO KNOW THAT THERE ARE SO MANY DIFFERENCES TO UNDERSTAND, TOLERATE, AND INTEGRATE.

■

GALISTEO NEWS, SANTA FE, N.M.

WHAT IS PENIS ENVY, AND HOW DID SIGMUND FREUD THINK HE KNEW SOMETHING ABOUT IT IF HE'S A MAN?

SIGMUND FREUD WAS UNCONSCIOUSLY PROJECTING. HE REALLY MEANT THAT ALL MEN HAVE *BREAST* ENVY. HE KNEW THIS BECAUSE HE WOULD, AT THE HEIGHT OF HIS COCAINE INTOXICATION, SPEND HOURS AT THE DAY'S END IN FRONT OF HIS MIRROR, TRYING ON BRASSIERE CAMISOLES. THIS IS AN AS YET UNPUBLISHED FACT, FOUND IN THE DIARIES OF CARL JUNG'S MAID. OF COURSE, THERE IS ANOTHER THEORY: THAT PENIS ENVY IS SOMETHING THAT DOES NOT BELONG TO WOMEN BUT TO OTHER *MEN* TOWARD OTHER MEN. MEN *DO* CHECK EACH OTHER OUT IN PUBLIC URINALS, AND NOT ALWAYS FOR SALACIOUS REASONS ONLY!

THE VILLAGE VOICE, N.Y.C.

**THIS COLLEAGUE OF MINE TREATS WOMEN
LIKE DIRT, AND HE GETS ALL THE CHICKS.
I'M A GENTLEMAN, AND IT HURTS. WHERE'S
THE JUSTICE IN THAT?**

WHOEVER TOLD YOU THERE WAS JUSTICE IN LIFE, M'DEAR?
THERE ARE ONLY FACTS, AND THE FACT IS, WOMEN ARE AS
HABITUATED TO NEANDERTHAL, DRAG-ME-BY-THE-HAIR
MEN AS MEN ARE TO TITS-AND-ASS WOMEN. HABITS ARE
HARD TO UNRAVEL, BUT HANG IN THERE: A FEW WOMEN
HAVE JUST ABOUT KICKED THEIR ANCIENT ADDICTION TO
APEMEN.

SHAKESPEARE & CO., N.Y.C.

WHY DO MEN HAVE NIPPLES?

NIPPLES ON MEN ARE A REMINDER THAT THE FIRST SEX OF
ALL OF US IS FEMALE (THE EMBRYO IS *NOT* NEUTRAL IN THE
FIRST SIX WEEKS; IT'S *FEMALE*). ALSO, MEN HAVE NIPPLES
BECAUSE EVEN MEN ENJOY BEING SUCKLED FROM TIME TO
TIME. I UNDERSTAND THAT THERE IS AN AFRICAN TRIBE
THAT HAS MEN WHO CAN PRODUCE MILK; STRANGE AS
THIS SEEMS, 'TIS TRUE—A FURTHER REMINDER OF THE
FEMALENESS OF BOTH GENDERS.

GALISTEO NEWS, SANTA FE, N.M.

WHY DO WOMEN FIND IT NECESSARY TO SHARE THEIR FEMININE PROBLEMS WITH THE MALE PERSUASION?

PERHAPS THEY WANT TO INITIATE YOU INTO THE SECRETS WOMEN HAVE KEPT FOR SO LONG. IT SEEMS TO ME THAT ACQUAINTANCE WITH THESE "FEMININE PROBLEMS" CAN ASSIST YOU IN YOUR RELATIONSHIPS, BOTH SEXUAL AND NOT, WITH WOMEN. THE MORE YOU KNOW ABOUT "FEMININE PROBLEMS," THE MORE YOU'LL UNDERSTAND ABOUT THE FEMININE NATURE; AS A RESULT, THE NATURE OF YOUR OWN MALENESS WILL BECOME CLEARER, IN JUXTAPOSITION. ONCE THE DIFFERENCES ARE SEEN, ACCEPTANCE OF, AND RESPECT FOR, THE DIFFERENCES CAN GROW.

SHAKESPEARE & CO., N.Y.C.

WHY CAN'T MY FEMALE FRIEND MAKE MONEY?

THE MONEY GAME IS A WAR GAME, AND WAR IS NOT A WOMAN'S EVENT. NOR IS COMPETITION, ANOTHER MAJOR COMPONENT OF THE MONEY GAME. WERE MONEY TO BE USED IN A NURTURING WAY, MORE FOR CARE OF THE POPULACE THAN FOR PURCHASE OF POWER, YOUR FEMALE FRIEND WOULD KNOW HOW TO MAKE MONEY: MAKE MONEY WORK FOR THE RIGHT OF ALL TO LIFE, LIBERTY, AND THE PURSUIT OF PURPOSE.

GALISTEO NEWS, SANTA FE, N.M.

WHY DO AMERICAN MEN FEAR COMMITMENT?

HONEY, HAVE *YOU* EVER BEEN COMMITTED? IT'S NO LIGHTWEIGHT EXPERIENCE, THE STRAITJACKETS OF COMMITMENT! PERHAPS WE NEED TO SEPARATE THE THOUGHT OF "RELATIONSHIP" FROM THE WORD "COMMITMENT," GIVEN THE INSANE ASYLUM MEANING OF THE WORD, YES??

■

GALISTEO NEWS, SANTA FE, N.M.

AHH, THE BOYS! MEN—THEY ALWAYS SEEM SO IMPOSSIBLE. HOW DOES ONE LIVE WITH THEM?

PATIENTLY.

THE GAMUT, SANTA FE, N.M.

WOMEN ARE THE ONLY CREATURES IN THE WORLD WHO POSSESS AN ORGAN—THE CLITORIS—WHOSE SOLE PURPOSE IS SEXUAL GRATIFICATION. PLEASE COMMENT.

WOMEN ARE MADE FOR LOVING. THE ANCIENT CHINESE KNEW THIS. THEY MADE AN ART OF KEEPING THEIR WIVES PLEASURED. THE ANCIENT CHINESE MAN VISITED HIS WIFE SEVERAL TIMES A DAY TO STOKE HER EROTIC EMBERS. HE KNEW THAT LOVING ATTENTION GENERATES FROM A WOMAN THE LOVING ATTENTION *HE* DESIRES. A WELL-LOVED WOMAN HOLDS UP THE MIRROR OF GREATNESS TO HER MAN. SHE IS FILLED WITH FRUITS THAT NOURISH HER LOVER. THE UNIQUENESS OF WOMAN'S SEXUAL PHYSIQUE PROVES THAT LOVING IS THE ANSWER TO THE RIDDLE OF HOW TO KEEP HER DOWN ON THE FARM.

■

STAGHORN, N.Y.C.

WHY CAN'T MEN OPEN UP?

LOOK TO BIOLOGY FOR THE ANSWER. INNATELY, WOMEN'S FUNCTION IS TO OPEN, WHILE MEN'S INNATE FUNCTION IS TO SPEAR/PIERCE/SKEWER. ALSO, HISTORICALLY, IT HAS BEEN MEN'S WORK TO FIGHT, KILL, MAKE WAR AND ENE-MIES. ONE CANNOT BE OPEN OF MIND, SOUL, OR EMO-TIONS WHEN THE JOB IS THUS. MEN HAVE HAD TO

OPERATE BEHIND SHIELDS AND ARMOR FOREVER, AND THIS SHIELDING HAS BECOME ENCODED GENETICALLY. NOW HUMANITY IS STRIVING TO BALANCE THE ONE-SIDEDNESS OF OUR GENDERS, TO BRING THE SOFT, FEELINGFUL NATURE OF THE FEMININE INTO PLAY IN THE MALE "COSTUME" AND THE FOCUSING OF THE MASCULINE INTO THE FEMALE'S "COSTUME." (I THINK OF GENDER AS A "COSTUME" THE SOUL ENTERS EACH LIFETIME IN ORDER TO FULFILL ITS GROWTH POTENTIAL. IF MORE MEN AND WOMEN LOOKED AT THEIR GENDER THAT WAY, THEY WOULD NOT GET SO ATTACHED TO BEHAVING IN ONLY ONE MODE, NOR WOULD THEY GET SO INSULTED WHEN THE GENDER THEY WEAR IS CRITICIZED.)

■

GALISTEO NEWS, SANTA FE, N.M.

IS BISEXUALITY SOME FORM OF PAST-LIFE KARMA? MUST I GO THROUGH SUCH PAINFUL CHANGES BECAUSE OF IT? A LOT OF BISEXUAL PEOPLE I KNOW ARE GOING THROUGH DESTRUCTIVE CHANGES.

BISEXUALITY IS THE REAL NATURE OF EVERYTHING, FOR INTERTWINED THROUGHOUT NATURE IS THE INTERMINGLING OF OPPOSITES, OF THE MALE AND THE FEMALE, THE LIGHT AND THE DARK, THE STRAIGHT AND THE CURVED. HOWEVER, WE HUMANS HAVE THE GENDERS NEATLY

DIVIDED INTO SPECIFIC ROLES, WITH STRICTURES AND LAWS TO MAINTAIN THESE ROLES. BISEXUALITY ISN'T REALLY YOUR PROBLEM, I THINK, SO MUCH AS IS YOUR ATTEMPT TO FIT YOUR TRUE FEELINGS INTO THE NARROW NOOKS OF SOCIETY'S RULES. YOU HAVE TO FIND THE COURAGE TO BELIEVE IN YOURSELF AND LIVE THIS BELIEF. IT'S NOT EASY TO BE AN ICONOCLAST, AN EVOLUTIONARY IF YOU WILL, BUT WHEN YOU ARE ONE, YOU HAVE TWO CHOICES: EXPRESS IT AND SUFFER THE OUTER WORLD'S CENSURE, OR SUPPRESS IT AND SUFFER AN INNER-WORLD CANCER. BY EXPRESSING YOUR TRUE NATURE, YOU BECOME A TEACHER BY EXAMPLE TO THE PORTION OF HUMANITY BEING HELD HOSTAGE BY SOCIETY'S NORMS.

■

GALISTEO NEWS, SANTA FE, N.M.

WHY DO MEN TURN HOMOSEXUAL WHEN THERE ARE WOMEN?

MANY REASONS:

—SCIENCE HAS DISCOVERED THAT IT IS A CHEMICAL CON-STITUENCY OF THE WOMAN'S WOMB DURING PREGNANCY. —METAPHYSICIANS SAY IT IS BECAUSE THE SOUL IS MAK-ING A TRANSITION FROM ONE GENDER TO THE OTHER AND IS RELUCTANT TO DO SO. —HOMOSEXUAL MEN SAY THAT HOMOSEXUALITY IS THE *TRUE* NATURE OF MALE SEX-

UALITY. —PSYCHOLOGISTS OFTEN SAY IT'S BECAUSE THE MOTHER OVERSHADOWED THE FATHER, OR THE FATHER WAS NEVER THERE TO GIVE LOVE OR EXAMPLE. —FEMINISTS WHO HAVE COMPASSION SAY IT'S BECAUSE THESE MEN WHO PREFER MEN ARE RUNNING AWAY FROM THE ANGER OF WOMEN. —I SAY IT'S BECAUSE MEN HAVE A LOT IN COMMON, ESPECIALLY SEXUALITY. MEN WANT "IT" MORE THAN WOMEN DO (GENERALLY) AND MORE RAWLY TOO, SO WHO BETTER FOR MEN TO GO TO FOR RELEASE OF THEIR MOST BASIC NEED THAN OTHER MEN? HOMOSEXUALITY IN HUMANS HAS ALWAYS BEEN; THE WOMEN OF THE ORIENTAL WORLD WERE MADE LOVE TO BY THEIR HANDMAIDENS WHEN THEIR MATES WERE AWAY, AND EVEN PROVIDED WITH JADE STALKS (KNOWN TODAY IN THEIR PLASTIC REINCARNATION AS DILDOS); WHILE WARRIORS OF EVERY CULTURE HAVE HAD SEXUAL ENCOUNTERS WITH EACH OTHER. IN OTHER WORDS, MEN TURN HOMOSEXUAL FOR THE SAME REASON RAIN TURNS TO SNOW: A CHANGE IN CONDITIONS.

GALISTEO NEWS, SANTA FE, N.M.

WHY DO PEOPLE HAVE SEX?

TO COMMUNICATE TOTALLY

TO FEEL DELICIOUS

TO TOUCH DEEPLY

TO RELEASE

AND CONNECT.

BUT SOME PEOPLE HAVE SEX

TO SATISFY AN ITCH

BECAUSE THEIR LINGAM GETS ERECT

BECAUSE THEY'RE BEING PAID

BECAUSE THEY'RE MARRIED AND IT'S THERE

TO ENTRAP THE PARTNER

TO HAVE CHILDREN

TO FILL TIME

TO SATISFY CURIOSITY

BECAUSE IT'S THE "THING" TO DO

BECAUSE THEIR FATHER PAID FOR IT

BECAUSE IT'S FORBIDDEN.

AND WE *ALL* HAVE SEX BECAUSE NO MATTER HOW OR

WHY SEX IS EXPERIENCED, IT'S *ALWAYS* THE BEST FUN ON

EARTH.

THE GAMUT, SANTA FE, N.M.

**IS IT POSSIBLE TO HAVE GOOD SEX FOR
TWENTY YEARS?**

NOT WITHOUT A BREAK.

■

GALISTEO NEWS, SANTA FE, N.M.

**MY LAST LOVER HAS A MASSIVE MIDDLE. OUR
LAST TIME TOGETHER, I THREW HIM OFF,
AND I'M AFRAID I WOUNDED HIM HORRIBLY. I
THINK OF HIM CONSTANTLY AND CAN'T GET
HIM BACK. WHAT CAN I DO?**

WAIT IT OUT. YOU'RE JUST EXPERIENCING AURA GAP:
YOUR AURIC FIELD HAS BEEN VACATED BY ITS MOST
RECENT, CLOSEST TENANT. ANYWAY, PEOPLE WITH MAS-
SIVE MIDDLES ARE MORE INTERESTED IN ERECTING A
FORTRESS AROUND THEMSELVES THAN IN OPENING TO
INTIMACY.

■

THE VILLAGE VOICE, N.Y.C.

**WHY DO PEOPLE HAVE TWO OF EVERYTHING
EXCEPT A PENIS AND VAGINA? SERIOUSLY.**

IT WAS THE CREATOR'S WAY OF REMINDING US THAT IT
TAKES TWO, AND ONLY TWO, TO DO THE TANGO OF LOVE.
SERIOUSLY.

GERANIUM SLIP, SANTA FE, N.M.

SHOULD I, A MALE, BE AGGRESSIVE OR PASSIVE DURING THE SEXUAL MATING GAME?

YES, IN ALTERNATING RHYTHMS. YOU WILL GET THE MOST OUT OF THE SEXUAL MATING GAME BY AGGRESSIVELY TURNING YOUR PARTNER ON AND PASSIVELY RECEIVING THE ENERGY SHE SURROUNDS YOU WITH.

THE VILLAGE VOICE, N.Y.C.

WHAT'S LOVE GOT TO DO WITH IT?

NOT ENOUGH!

THE GAMUT, SANTA FE, N.M.

DO YOU SMOKE AFTER YOU MAKE LOVE?

IF THE FIRE'S BEEN LIT DURING, YES.

GALISTEO NEWS, SANTA FE, N.M.

WHY DON'T MORE WOMEN APPRECIATE THE BEAUTY OF THE MALE SEX ORGANS?

JEALOUSY. IN THIS REGARD, FREUD WAS RIGHT: THE FEMALE'S SEXUAL APPARATUS ISN'T *NEARLY* AS EXQUISITELY BEAUTIFUL AS THE MALE'S. THAT'S WHY WE CELEBRATE THE LINGAM (HINDI FOR PENIS) IN OUR SKYSCRAPERS AND SPIRES. ONCE, THOUGH, WE HAD

HOGANS, CAVES THAT EMULATED THE COMFORTING HOME OF WOMB, WHEREIN PEOPLE WORSHIPED. BUT THAT WAS LONG AGO, WHEN RESPECT AND AWE FOR MOTHER AND BIRTH STILL WAS.

■

THE GAMUT, SANTA FE, N.M.

IS "CLIT" A VERB OR NOUN? ACTIVE OR PASSIVE, PAST OR PRESENT?

WHEN STIMULATED, "CLIT" IS A VERB, ACTIVE AND PRESENT. WHEN IGNORED, AS SO OFT IT IS, IT'S A PASSIVE, PAST NOUN. HERE'S TO KEEPING IT A VERB, DEARIE. PLEASE GET INSTRUCTION IN HOW.

■

HUDSON STREET PAPERS, N.Y.C.

WHY DO SOME WOMEN SAY TO MEN, "MAKE LOVE *TO* ME!" INSTEAD OF "MAKE LOVE *WITH* ME!"?

PERHAPS BECAUSE THE PROBLEM REALLY *IS* THAT THE MAN NEEDS TO MAKE LOVE *TO* HER INSTEAD OF *WITH* HER. MANY MEN TODAY HAVE FORGOTTEN THE COMMUNICATIONS OF TEN YEARS AGO ABOUT THE NATURE OF WOMEN'S ANATOMY AND THE WAY SHE CLIMAXES TO ORGASM.

COLLEGE OF SANTA FE, SANTA FE, N.M.

DOES GOOD ART COME FROM GOOD SEX, OR DOES GOOD SEX COME FROM THE EXTENSION OF CREATIVE THINKING?

GOOD SEX IS NOT REQUIRED FOR GOOD ART TO MANIFEST; BUT CREATIVE THINKING IS THE *ONLY* WAY TO GOOD SEX.

■

HUDSON STREET PAPERS, N.Y.C.

SEX LIFE AT HOME GETTING BORING, SEX LIFE ELSEWHERE GETTING BORING. WHERE NEXT?

LAY OFF, SO TO SPEAK; REST. MAYBE YOU NEED TO CONSIDER YOUR "SEX" LIFE AS A "LOVE" LIFE. LEARN ABOUT SEX AS A COMMUNICATION OF ENERGY, AS A WAY OF MELDING SOUL TO SOUL. LEARN THE TANTRIC APPROACH. THERE ARE SOME VERY GOOD BOOKS OUT NOW DESCRIBING THE EASTERN TECHNIQUES FOR RAISING CONSCIOUSNESS THROUGH SEXLOVE. IN THE MEANTIME, WHILE YOU'RE BORED, EXPERIENCE LIFE WITHOUT SEXUAL RELEASE FOR A WHILE. YOU MAY EVEN GET MORE CREATIVE WORK DONE, AND CERTAINLY YOU'LL ESTABLISH A DIFFERENT KIND OF RELATING WITH THOSE WHO ARE THE OBJECTS OF YOUR SEXUAL DELIGHT.

GALISTEO NEWS, SANTA FE, N.M.

WHY OH WHY DOES IT EXCITE ME SO WHEN A LITTLE OL' FLY CRAWLS UP MY LEG? —"A Neurotic Female Talking About Love"

DEAR NEUROTIC FEMALE TALKING ABOUT LOVE:
PERHAPS YOU NEED TO SAY "YES" MORE OFTEN; CHECK OUT A FEW LARGER FLIES AND THEIR CONTENTS: SURVEY, SEDUCE, AND SUCCUMB.

■

GALISTEO NEWS, SANTA FE, N.M.

DEAR LADY: WHAT IS MORE FUN, LAUGHTER OR SEX?

YOU'VE BEEN CELIBATE TOO LONG, M'THINKS!

■

STAGHORN, N.Y.C.

WHY IS IT THAT WHEN WOMEN SUCCUMB TO THE PLEASURES OF SEX ON THE FIRST DATE, THE MAN NO LONGER HAS A SERIOUS INTEREST? ARE WE TO FOREVER PLAY GAMES?

THE VIRGIN HABIT HAS NOT BEEN SHED FROM THE MINDS OF MEN. THEY LIKE THE HUNT. AFTER THE KILL, THEY'RE OUT STALKING NEW DEARS TO ADD TO THEIR TROPHY ROOM. WHEN IS WOMAN GOING TO LEARN TO TAKE THE MAN, AMAZON LIKE, FOR HER PLEASURE AND LET HIM GO WHEN SHE'S SATED? DOES WOMAN REALLY NEED MAN HANGING AROUND THE HOUSE ASKING FOR COFFEE AND

HEAD ALL DAY? ON THE OTHER SIDE OF THIS COIN, WHY ARE WOMEN STANDING NAKED AND OPEN ON THE FIRST DATE ANYMORE? DOESN'T WOMAN WANT TO KNOW THE SOUL OF THE PERSON SHE TAKES INTO HER BODY? SHE DOESN'T HAVE THE ROYAL ITCH AS STRONGLY AS MEN DO, SO THERE IS MORE EASE FOR WOMAN IN THE GETTING-TO-KNOW-YOU DANCE. THIS TIME-TAKING WILL ALSO INTRIGUE THE EVER-HUNTING MALE. TO MAN'S VIRGIN GAME, WOMAN PLAYS THE WIFE GAME. BOTH ARE OUT-DATED. MUTATE NOW, AVOID THE RUSH.

■

GALISTEO NEWS, SANTA FE, N.M.

ISN'T SEX GOOD FOR THE SOUL?
(IT SEEMS APPARENT THAT IT IS.)

OH, YES, SEX IS GOOD FOR THE SOUL, SEX THAT COMMU-NICATES, SEX THAT MELTS AND BLENDS PARTNERS. WE HUMANS HAVE BEEN UNCOMFORTABLE WITH SEX FOR ALL OF OUR RECORDED HISTORY. EVEN THE TIBETAN TANTRICS, SO FAMOUS FOR THEIR SEXUAL PRACTICES, CAST THE SEXUAL SIDE OF THEIR TEACHINGS INTO THE BACK STREETS OF ILL REPUTE, GIVING ALL CREDENCE TO "WHITE" TANTRA AND HIDING THE "RED" TANTRA OF SEX-UAL RITUALS. BY CALLING SEX EVIL, WE HAVE RAISED THE OTHER SIDE OF THE ENERGY—VIOLENCE—TO EXTREME HEIGHTS AND TURNED WHAT WE *DO* IN SEX EITHER TO

PROCREATIVE WEDLOCK OR TO KINKY VASELINE DEBAUCHES. IT'S GOOD TO SEE A "NORMAL," MIDCOUNTRY, MIDDLE-CLASS YOUNG WOMAN BE *SPIRITUALLY* DELIGHTED WITH SEX!

∎

GALISTEO NEWS, SANTA FE, N.M.

WHY CAN'T I, A GOOD-LOOKING, INTELLECTUAL, WITTY, PERSONABLE, FUNNY, ASTUTE, LONELY MAN, GET LAID?

WOMEN NO LONGER WANT TO GET LAID:

THEY WANT TO GET LOVED.

∎

GALISTEO NEWS, SANTA FE, N.M.

HOW DOES ONE MAKE LOVE TO A WOMAN?

WITH CLITORAL KISSES AND CARESSES, NIPPLE NIBBLING TOO, BEFORE PENETRATION AND FOR A LONG TIME, UNTIL EXPLOSION IS . . . THEN ENTER DEEPLY.

∎

GALISTEO NEWS, SANTA FE, N.M.

WHY DO WOMEN FAKE THEIR ORGASMS?

IT'S EASIER THAN TRYING TO PENETRATE THE MALE EGO TO TEACH HIM HOW TO CREATE A TRUE ORGASM IN WOMAN.

B. DALTON, N.Y.C.

WHEN AM I GOING TO MEET THE MAN OF MY DREAMS?

THE NEXT TIME YOU GO TO SLEEP!

■

THE VILLAGE VOICE, N.Y.C.

DOES THE PERFECT PERSON EXIST?

SURELY THERE MUST BE ONE TUCKED AWAY IN SOME SECLUDED CAVE IN THE EAST, INSTRUCTING OTHER SOULS IN THE ART OF PERFECTING. THERE *ARE*, THOUGH, MANY PERFECT*ING* PEOPLE IN EXISTENCE; THEY ARE SCATTERED THROUGHOUT THE WORLD, EVEN THROUGHOUT OHIO. THERE ARE, HOWEVER, NO PERFECT*ING* PEOPLE IN DETROIT.

GALISTEO NEWS, SANTA FE, N.M.

MY GIRLFRIENDS SUGGEST WEARING A CRYSTAL TO BED WHEN I SLEEP WITH SOMEONE. IS THIS SAFE? COULD OUR COMBINED AND AMPLIFIED ENERGIES BE FATAL?

WELL, WHAT THE HELL, ONE STEP FORWARD FOR EXPERIENCE! SEX AND DEATH ARE ALWAYS ASSOCIATED WITH EACH OTHER; PERHAPS IN THIS NEW-AGE PREVIEW TIME OF CRYSTALS NOW, APOCALYPSE TOMORROW, THIS LAST FRONTIER MUST BE CROSSED. YOU COULD WORK OUT QUITE AN ATTRACTIVE AND UNIQUE EUTHANASIA SERVICE IF ALL AMPLIFIES WELL!

THE GAMUT, SANTA FE, N.M.

DEAR MADAME BLAVATSKY: WILL I HAVE A MEANINGFUL RELATIONSHIP WITH THE GIRL I AM PRESENTLY GOING OUT WITH?

ASK YOURSELF THESE THINGS: WHAT DO YOU DEFINE AS A "MEANINGFUL" RELATIONSHIP? HOW MUCH TIME DO YOU ENJOY WITH HER, I MEAN *TRULY* ENJOY? WOULD YOU LOVE HER IF SHE SUDDENLY HAD AN ACCIDENT AND LOST ONE TIT AND HAD A SCAR ACROSS HER FACE? AND, IF YOU ARE NOT OVER THIRTY-EIGHT, I DO NOT THINK YOU, AS A MAN, ARE READY FOR A MEANINGFUL RELATIONSHIP!

COLLEGE OF SANTA FE, SANTA FE, N.M.

WHY DO NICE GUYS FINISH LAST?

THEY'RE TOO CONCERNED WITH THE FEELINGS OF OTH-
ERS TO DO THE OBNOXIOUS ROUTINE IT TAKES TO PUSH
THROUGH COMPETITION. COMPETITION IS A STRANGE
BEAST. HOW HUMANE CAN YOU BE WHEN YOUR MOTIVE
IS TO BE "BETTER THAN" SOMEONE? NICE GUYS ARE TRY-
ING TO BE BETTER THAN THEY ARE, NOT BETTER THAN
SOMEONE.

■

GALISTEO NEWS, SANTA FE, N.M.

I JUST GOT LAID OFF FOR A WEEK. I CAN'T FIND A SKIRT WHO WILL SPEND ANY TIME WITH ME. NO BAR IN THIS TOWN SEEMS TO HAVE DRAFT BEER. THIS TOWN ISN'T WORTH A SHIT.

BUT THE SKY IS BRILLIANTLY CLEAR AND BLUE, THE SUN-
SETS ARE SPECTACULAR, AND THE LIVIN' IS EASY. . . .

GALISTEO NEWS, SANTA FE, N.M.

WHY IS IT I END UP IN BED WITH A WOMAN I ONLY INTENDED TO BE FRIENDS WITH AND THE SEX WAS GREAT?

YOU WERE READY FOR A QUANTUM JUMP IN THE HAY!

■

GALISTEO NEWS, SANTA FE, N.M.

WHY IS LOVING SO HARD?

ERRONEOUS INSTRUCTIONS.

■

GALISTEO NEWS, SANTA FE, N.M.

IS LOVE NECESSARILY NARCISSISTIC?

ONLY FOR MEN, WHO ARE USED TO LOVING THE GODLIKE REFLECTION WOMEN HAVE BEEN GIVING THEM FOR EONS. FROM ANOTHER POINT OF VIEW, NOT MANY HUMANS ON THE PLANET TODAY ADMIRE THEMSELVES, NO LESS LOVE THEMSELVES; SO WE END UP IN A REVERSE OF NARCISSISM, LOVING THE PROJECTION OF WHAT WE *THINK* WE SHOULD BE, IN THE CHARACTER OF OUR LOVER, AND LETTING OUR TRUE SELF WITHER ON THE VINE OF DENIAL.

GALISTEO NEWS, SANTA FE, N.M.

CAN YOU DEFINE THE RELATIONSHIP
BETWEEN MEN AND WOMEN?

AN INTERACTION OF COMPLEMENTARY OPPOSITES THAT
REQUIRES CONTINUAL ADJUSTMENT TO KEEP THE OPPOSI-
TION FROM OVERRIDING THE COMPLEMENTARITY.

■

GALISTEO NEWS, SANTA FE, N.M.

PLEASE GIVE SOME COMFORTING WORDS TO
A SCARED LITTLE GIRL TRAPPED IN A SECURE
GROWING WOMAN'S REALITY.

IN THE "ING" IS THE "ZING" TO TAKE YOUR MIND FROM
THE FEAR AND VISION OF TRAP. IT'S IN THE VERB THAT
YOU'LL FIND VERVE.

■

GALISTEO NEWS, SANTA FE, N.M.

WILL HE STILL WANT ME WHEN I GET BACK?

SURE. BUT WILL HE WANT YOU AFTER
YOU'VE *BEEN THERE* AWHILE?

HUDSON STREET PAPERS, N.Y.C.

**WHY DOES IT SEEM THAT ALL THE BOYS ON
MY SWIM TEAM LIKE ME? CAN YOU HELP ME
TRY TO UNDERSTAND THAT FEELING?**
(Asked by a fifteen-year-old girl)

THE BOYS ARE BEING "TURNED ON" BY PUBERTY AND THE
ONSET OF NEW CHEMICAL REACTIONS. YOUR SWEET
YOUNG BODY IN A BATHING SUIT STIRS UP THESE CHEMI-
CAL REACTIONS. FOR BOYS, THE *VISUAL* EVENT IS A PHYSI-
CAL TURN-ON; FOR GIRLS, THE MENTAL/EMOTIONAL
QUALITIES OF BOYS ARE MORE IMPORTANT. YOU'RE ON
THE RIGHT TRACK WHEN YOU ASK FOR HELP IN UNDER-
STANDING BOYS' REACTIONS TO YOU: THERE'S A LOT TO
BE LEARNED ABOUT THE DIFFERENCES BETWEEN FEMALES
AND MALES.

■

GALISTEO NEWS, SANTA FE, N.M.

**HOW OLD SHOULD YOU BE WHEN
YOU FIRST GET LAYED?**
(Asked by a thirteen-year-old boy)

OLD ENOUGH TO BE ATTRACTED TO SOMEONE WHO CAN
TEACH YOU THE WAYS, MEANS, AND COMMUNICATION
PURPOSE OF "GETTING LAID."

CARDS & SUCH, FOREST HILLS, N.Y.

WHAT DO I DO WHEN I HAVE AN AFFAIR WITH MY BEST FRIEND'S MOTHER?
(Asked by a sixteen-year-old boy)

YOU LEARN AS MUCH AS YOU CAN, AND ARE GRATEFUL FOR THE LOVE TEACHINGS OF AN OLDER WOMAN—EVERY YOUNG MAN NEEDS THEM. AND YOU DON'T GO ANNOUNCING IT ALL OVER THE BLOCK, EITHER! IF YOUR BEST FRIEND DOESN'T KNOW BY NOW, "SOUND HIM OUT" TENDERLY FOR HOW HE'LL HANDLE THE NEWS. IF YOU PERCEIVE THAT HE *CAN'T* DEAL WITH IT, DON'T FORCE IT ON HIM. ABOVE ALL, RESPECT THIS WOMAN FOR THE WISDOM AND EXPERIENCE SHE CAN GIVE YOU.

■

GALISTEO NEWS, SANTA FE, N.M.

IF SPACE IS LOVE, THEN IS LOVE SPACE, AND IF TIME EATS THE DOUGHNUT, DOES LOVE EAT THE HOLE?

LOVE IS MORE A FIELD THAT NEEDS SPACE TO LIVE, AND LOVE DEVOURS THE HOLE TO MAKE ONE WHOLE, BUT LEAVES A HOLE WHEN ITS FLOWERS DIE.

GALISTEO NEWS, SANTA FE, N.M.

IN A CYNICAL SOCIETY, TO BE HAPPY YOU MUST POSSESS IRONY WITH LOVE AS IF IT WERE WHAT?

HOPE.

■

GALISTEO NEWS, SANTA FE, N.M.

WHY CAN'T FREE SOULS MAKE A COMMITMENT?

THEY ALREADY HAVE—TO FREEDOM-TO-BE.

■

ZIA DINER, SANTA FE, N.M.

WHAT IS THE RELATIONSHIP BETWEEN COMMITMENT AND PLEASURE?

RARE!

■

HUDSON STREET PAPERS, N.Y.C.

WHY DOESN'T LOVE CONQUER ALL?

IT DOES, WHEN IT'S PURE. TROUBLE IS, WE HUMANS ARE SO DENSE WE INSIST ON LACING OUR LOVE WITH EXPEC-TATIONS, POSSESSIONS, OWNERSHIP, NEED: MAKES A BIT-TER BREW, GUARANTEED TO GIVE RISE TO HEARTBURN.

HUDSON STREET PAPERS, N.Y.C.

DOES LOVE ALWAYS CAUSE PAIN, AND IF NOT, HOW DO YOU GO ABOUT FINDING LOVE WITHOUT PAIN?

DARLING, DARLING, DARLING—IT IS NOT *LOVE* THAT CAUSES PAIN! LOVE IS PURE BLISS. *ATTACHMENT* CAUSES PAIN. LET GO, AND YOU WILL HAVE LOVE WITHOUT PAIN.

■

HUDSON STREET PAPERS, N.Y.C.

WHAT DO MEN REALLY WANT? WHAT DO WOMEN REALLY WANT? AND WHY?

WOMEN REALLY WANT TO HOLD. MEN REALLY WANT TO PIERCE. THE BIOLOGY MAKES IT SO. WOMEN ARE THE CLEFT MOON, MEN THE SHOOTING ARROW. WOMEN ARE BUOYING WATER; MEN ARE SEARING FLAMES YEARNING TO BURN THROUGH TO FREEDOM.

■

GALISTEO NEWS, SANTA FE, N.M.

WHERE IS THE BEST PLACE TO ENJOY SEX?

IN YOUR MIND, WHICH SEEMS TO APPRECIATE OPEN FIELDS AND CANDLELIT BEDROOMS.

HUDSON STREET PAPERS, N.Y.C.

CAN LOVE MAKE US HEALTHIER? SMARTER? SEXIER? RICHER?

YES, THROUGH THE CARESS OF BLISS AND THE PENETRATION OF PAIN, ONE WAY OR BOTH, LOVE IS THE MOST INFORMATIVE TEACHER WE GET.

LOVE MAKES US HEALTHIER BY FORCING US TO SEE OURSELVES AT OUR MOST VULNERABLE; BY GOADING US TO MEND OUR FISSURES AND BEND OUR PATTERNS; BY IMBUING US WITH INCANDESCENT, GLOWING *WILL-TO-LIVE*.

LOVE MAKES US SMARTER BY ENTICING AND PUSHING US TO KNOW OURSELVES BETTER, TO WANT TO DO MORE IN LIFE. LOVE OF COURSE MAKES US SEXIER BY INSPIRING US TO WANT TO GET CLOSER TO THE LOVER.

LOVE MAKES US RICHER IN OUR PERSON; AND CAN EQUALLY PROVOKE ONE TO INCREASE THE MATERIAL COMFORTS FOR THE SAKE OF THE LIFE OF THE LOVE.

■

GALISTEO NEWS, SANTA FE, N.M.

WHAT IS LOVE? HOW CAN I GET SOME?

LOVE IS A FIELD. YOU CAN GET INTO THAT FIELD BY FINE TUNING; USUALLY THIS TUNING IS DONE WITH THE HELP OF ANOTHER, WITH WHOM WE RESONATE: A PARENT, A CHILD, A LOVER, A MATE, A TEACHER, A MANTRA.

HUDSON STREET PAPERS, N.Y.C.

I'M GETTING MARRIED IN FIVE DAYS. DO YOU HAVE ANY ADVICE FOR ME?

AS KAHLIL GIBRAN ADVISED, "LET THERE BE SPACES IN YOUR TOGETHERNESS."* REMEMBER THAT LOVE IS FOR YOUR GROWTH, NOT JUST FOR CUDDLES. REMEMBER THAT WHAT WOMAN WANTS IS *NOT* WHAT MAN WANTS; AND, REMEMBERING, RESEARCH THE DIFFERENCE THROUGH AWARENESS OF YOUR MATE, INTROSPECTION, WISE FRIENDS, AND LITERATURE. FOR CONFRONTATIONS AND AIRING OF DIFFICULT FEELINGS, KEEP A COMMON DIARY. WHEN YOU'RE PISSED, WRITE IT OUT. YOUR PARTNER CAN READ IT LATER, WHEN HE OR SHE IS READY AND YOU ARE OUT OF THE HEAT OF IT. YOUR SPOUSE CAN RESPOND IN THE DIARY TOO. THIS ALLEVIATES SCREAMING-BANSHEE ARGUMENTS AND PROVIDES A RECORD OF YOUR EARLY ADJUSTMENTS TO EACH OTHER; A RECORD YOU CAN CHUCKLE OVER IN CALMER TIMES.

*Kahlil Gibran, *The Prophet*. New York: Alfred A. Knopf, 1923.

ZIA DINER, SANTA FE, N.M.

THE HEART MAKES CHOICES THAT THE MIND CAN ONLY REJECT AS HAZARDOUS.

THE HEART IS THE TRUTH OF US, FOR BETTER OR FOR WORSE. THE MIND IS MERELY THE OBSERVANT LIBRARIAN, STORING TAPES FOR A JUDGMENT DAY.

■

GALISTEO NEWS, SANTA FE, N.M.

WHAT'S THE BEST VALENTINE'S GIFT A MAN CAN GIVE?

INTEREST IN, ATTENTION TO, HIS LOVED ONE: TOTAL FOCUS FOR THE DAY.

■

HUDSON STREET PAPERS, N.Y.C.

WHAT SHOULD A MAN DO IF HE IS IN LOVE WITH TWO WOMEN AT THE SAME TIME?

ASK HIMSELF: DOES HE REALLY HAVE THE EMOTIONAL, MENTAL, AND SEXUAL STAMINA TO CARE FOR *ONE* WOMAN, LET ALONE TWO? AND DOES HE HAVE THE SPIRITUAL DEPTH TO TOUCH SOULS EQUALLY WITH TWO ENTITIES IN SUCH A TOTAL MELD EXPERIENCE AS "LOVE" REQUIRES? CAN THE WOMEN HE LOVES ACCEPT THIS SITUATION? HE NEEDS TO EXAMINE HIS MOTIVES, HIS ABILITIES, AND THE FEEDBACK FROM HIS LOVES.

ZIA DINER, SANTA FE, N.M.

IS THERE SUCH A THING AS A WOMAN WHOSE RELATIONSHIPS ARE NOT COMPLETELY CONTROLLED BY FRIENDS AND THEIR EXPECTATIONS?

WOMEN TALK TO SORT OUT THEIR FEELINGS AND ACTIONS. WOMEN IN THE NINETIES ARE STRIDENT IN THEIR DEMANDS FOR EXCELLENT AND RESPECTFUL BEHAVIOR FROM MEN, AND THEIR WOMEN FRIENDS REMIND THEM TO BE STRONG. BUT YOU MAY FIND A WOMAN WHO WANTS TO CONFIDE IN NO ONE BUT YOU, SOMEWHERE IN THE BACKWOODS OF TENNESSEE. . . .

■

STAGHORN, N.Y.C.

WHY ARE ALL GOOD-LOOKING MEN EITHER GAY OR MARRIED?

THERE ARE MORE WOMEN IN THE WORLD THAN MEN AT THIS TIME. SINCE THE SINGLES SEX SCENE IS DANGEROUS THESE DAYS AND MEN'S SEXUAL NEED IS GREAT, THEY ARE MARRYING SOONER THAN LATER. AS TO BEING GAY, AN EX-LESBIAN SAID TO ME RECENTLY, "TO TELL YOU THE TRUTH, I PREFER MEN BECAUSE WOMEN ARE SO HARD TO DEAL WITH." WOMEN'S EMOTIONAL CLUTCH AND DEMANDS ARE TOO MUCH TO DEAL WITH IN A DECADE OF OUTER DIFFICULTY AND INNER TRANSFORMATION. SO,

MORE AND MORE MEN ARE OPTING FOR THEIR OWN REFLECTION, WHERE THEY CAN WORK OUT THE SENSITIZING OF THEIR NATURE IN SAFER EMOTIONAL TERRITORY. AND, WOMEN *ARE* LEARNING TO DETACH FROM THEIR CLUTCH-TO-BE-FILLED, TO TURN THEIR ATTENTION INSTEAD TO THE NURTURANCE OF THEIR OWN SELF, THEIR OWN LIFE AND TRUE WORK. BUT THEY'RE NOT LEARNING FAST ENOUGH. TOO MANY ARE STILL SAYING, "WHEN WILL I MEET *HIM*," AS IF THEIR ENTIRE EXISTENCE STILL DEPENDED ON MEETING A MAN AND MARRYING HIM.

■

HUDSON STREET PAPERS, N.Y.C.

WHAT DO YOU DO WHEN YOU CAN'T BE WITH THE ONE YOU LOVE?

BE WITH A FRIEND YOU LOVE, SHARE SUPPER AND A BOTTLE OF GOOD WINE. BE WITH YOURSELF. IN A BUBBLE BATH, PUT ON MUSIC AND DANCE NAKED AROUND THE HOUSE. WRITE A LETTER TO THE ONE YOU LOVE, OR CALL AND MAKE LOVE OVER THE PHONE. REMEMBER THAT *YOU'RE* THE ONE YOU LOVE, TOO, AND TREAT YOURSELF THUSLY.

THE GAMUT, SANTA FE, N.M.

HOW DO YOU HAVE LOVE WITHOUT ATTACHMENT?

BE AT THE POINT WHERE YOU KNOW YOU WANT NO
FETTERS ON YOUR OWN FREE FLOW; WHERE YOU KNOW
YOU WANT TO PUT NO FETTERS ON ANYONE ELSE'S FREE
FLOW.

WATCH:

BE AWARE

OF THE GRASP REACHING TO CLUTCH ONTO THE LOVER

WHO MAY WANT TO BE FREE TO EXPLORE WHAT HAS

COME ALONG, BE IT DINNER WITH FRIENDS OR A

ROMANTIC ESCAPADE.

IN THAT AWARENESS, REMEMBER YOUR LOVE

FOR THIS PERSON

AND HOW IT ENCOMPASSES CARE FOR THAT BEING'S

GROWTH AND JOY. REMEMBER YOUR OWN LOVE OF

FREELY FLOWING,

REMEMBER YOUR LOVE WITH EACH OTHER, GET TO THE

KERNEL OF IT,

FEEL ITS STRENGTH

AND KNOW

IT WILL NOT BREAK OR DWINDLE FROM THE LIGHTNESS

OF FREEDOM

BUT GROW.

HAVE CONVERSATIONS WITH THOSE PRACTICING THE ART
OF
LOVING WITHOUT ATTACHMENT,
FEED YOUR MIND WORDS OF WISDOM ON LOVING FREELY
AS FRIENDS.
IT TAKES WORK AND AWARENESS AND, ESPECIALLY, FED-
UPNESS WITH THE
PAINS OF ATTACHMENT-CAUSED JEALOUSY AND
EMOTIONAL TRAUMA TO BEGIN
TO LOVE WITHOUT ATTACHMENT.

■

THE GAMUT, SANTA FE, N.M.

WHY IS LOVE ASSOCIATED WITH THE HEART (AND NOT THE ANKLE)?

LOVE, LIKE THE HEART, KEEPS THE LIFE FORCE CIRCULAT-
ING. LOVE IS SOMETHING WE *FALL* INTO, AND LIKE
THE HEART, IT HAS A GREATER WAY *DOWN* IN ITS CIRCULA-
TION PROCESS (LOVE DELIVERS A GREATER FALL THAN
WE EXPECT). MAYBE WHEN WE LEARN TO LOVE WITH
MORE *UNDERSTANDING*, WE'LL ASSOCIATE THE ANKLE WITH
LOVING!

ZIA DINER, SANTA FE, N.M.

THE "BATTLE" BETWEEN MY "HEART" AND MY "HEAD" IS NEVER-ENDING, AND I TRUST NEITHER. WHERE CAN ONE GO, WHAT CAN ONE DO, TO END THIS EMOTIONAL WAR AND FIND PEACE AND BALANCE?

AS YOUR QUOTE MARKS INDICATE, YOU UNDERSTAND, THOUGH DIMLY, THAT THE HEART AND THE HEAD ARE YOU. YOU'VE SPLIT YOURSELF APART IN AN ATTEMPT TO DISOWN WHAT YOU FEAR SEEING OF YOURSELF. THE ONLY WAY TO LEARN, CHANGE, KNOW YOURSELF, IS TO LIVE YOURSELF OUT, RISK DOING WHAT YOU ARE. NO BLAME: WE WERE ALL TAUGHT TO BEHAVE WITHIN THE STRICTURE, NOT TO FREELY FLOW WITH OUR NATURE. MISTAKES PROVIDE THE WAY TO THE LIFE FULLY LIVED AND UNDERSTOOD.

GALISTEO NEWS, SANTA FE, N.M.

WHY WON'T MY PARENTS BUY ME A HORSE?

MANY REASONS:

THE JOB OF PARENTS IS NOT TO SATISFY BUT TO

FRUSTRATE YOUR WISHES, FOR THEY ARE TEACHING YOU

THE WAY OF THE WORLD;

IT'S DIFFICULT TO KEEP A HORSE IN A THREE-ROOM HOUSE;

HORSES ARE EXPENSIVE, AND SO IS THE HAY TO FEED THEM;

THEY KNOW YOUR SECRET WISH TO EMULATE LADY

GODIVA, EVEN IF YOU ARE OF THE MALE PERSUASION;

THEY ARE AFRAID YOU'LL SADDLE UP AND GALLOP AWAY

FROM THE HOMESTEAD;

THEY'RE ALLERGIC.

GALISTEO NEWS, SANTA FE, N.M.

IS IT MORAL TO HAVE SEX WITH SOMEONE YOU DON'T LOVE?

WHAT IS "MORAL"?

WHAT IS "LOVE"?

WHY ARE YOU THINKING ABOUT HAVING SEX WITH SOMEONE YOU THINK YOU DON'T "LOVE"?

TODAY, IT'S *STUPID*—NO, *IGNORANT*—TO HAVE SEX WITH SOMEONE YOU DON'T KNOW WELL ENOUGH TO "LOVE."

NOR IS IT THE OPTIMUM ARRANGEMENT FOR SEX.

IN THE DAYS OF THE MOTHER RELIGIONS, SEX WITH SOMEONE YOU DIDN'T "LOVE" WAS PART OF THE SPRING RELIGIOUS RITES; BUT MAKING THE SEX SACRED BROUGHT LOVE, A LESS PERSONAL LOVE, INTO PLAY. TO MY MIND, IF YOU'RE TURNED ON ENOUGH TO CONSIDER GETTING NAKED AND INTIMATE WITH A PERSON, THEN THERE IS "LOVE" BETWEEN YOU, LOVE BEING A FIELD OF *ATTRACTION*.

AS TO "MORAL," WHOSE MORALS ARE YOU GOING TO FOLLOW? WHILE YOU'RE DECIDING, HERE ARE SOME QUESTIONS FOR DECIDING WHETHER OR NOT SOMETHING IS "MORAL":

ARE YOU HURTING ANYONE, INCLUDING YOURSELF?

WHAT GOOD CAN YOU FORESEE FROM THE ACTION?

CAN YOU ENTER THE ACTION *CARING*?

WHOSE LIFE ARE YOU LIVING, ANYWAY?

GALISTEO NEWS, SANTA FE, N.M.

WHAT IS THE MATTER WITH BEING A ROMANTIC? WHY DO PEOPLE CALL IT "HOPELESS"?

OF ALL THINGS A ROMANTIC IS, IT ISN'T HOPELESS! *TOO* HOPEFUL, PERHAPS, AT LEAST WHERE ROMANCE IS APPLIED TO LOVE RELATIONSHIPS. ROMANCE, AS DEFINED BY *AMERICAN HERITAGE DICTIONARY*, IS "A LONG FICTITIOUS TALE OF . . . EXTRAORDINARY OR MYSTERIOUS EVENTS." THIS IS A WONDERFUL DEFINITION OF LOVE'S BEGINNING SPLENDOR, AN EXCELLENT RECIPE FOR BRINGING THE SEXUAL EXPERIENCE INTO MIND AS WELL AS BODY, AND AN EXCITING WAY TO IMAGINE THE FUTURE TOGETHER. BUT THE "HOPELESS" PART OF BEING A ROMANTIC OCCURS WHEN WE EXPECT THE REALITY TO BE AS HEROIC AS THE FICTION WE'VE IMAGINED. ROMANCE IS AN EXCELLENT VISUALIZATION TECHNIQUE BUT A LOUSY LIFE EXPECTATION.

SOCIETY

HUDSON STREET PAPERS, N.Y.C.

**WHATEVER
HAPPENED
TO COURAGE,
INTEGRITY, AND
INDIVIDUALITY
WITHOUT
COMMERCIAL
INTENT?**

WHO CAN AFFORD IT?

THE VILLAGE VOICE, N.Y.C.

HOW MANY ROACHES ARE THERE IN NEW YORK, AND WHERE DID THEY COME FROM?

THERE ARE SIXTY-SIX MILLION ROACHES OF THE CRAWLING KIND AND SIX MILLION OF THE SMOKING KIND. THEY BOTH ORIGINATED IN TROPICAL COUNTRIES.

GALISTEO NEWS, SANTA FE, N.M.

HOW CAN WE BE MORE LOVING TO ONE ANOTHER?

FORGIVE EVERYTHING.

THE GAMUT, SANTA FE, N.M.

WHY ARE SOME PEOPLE MEAN?
(Asked by an eight-year-old)

SOME PEOPLE HAVE HAD A MEAN LIFE, WITH NO ONE TO SHOW THEM LOVE OR MAKE THEM FEEL LOVED. THESE PEOPLE HAVE GROWN UP WITH THE SNOW KING AND QUEEN, PEOPLE OF ICY HEARTS, AND AS A RESULT THEIR OWN HEARTS HAVE TURNED TO ICE. MEAN PEOPLE NEED TO BE WARMED UP WITH UNDERSTANDING AND PATIENT, HONEST LOVING. CAN YOU UNDERSTAND PEOPLE WHO ARE MEAN TO YOU, CAN YOU FORGIVE THEM AND REMEMBER THAT THEY'RE MEAN BECAUSE THEY ARE IN PAIN?

GALISTEO NEWS, SANTA FE, N.M.

WHY DOES MY BROTHER HAVE
SHIT FOR BRAINS?

ARE YOU SURE IT'S NOT YOUR OWN SHIT YOU'RE

INTERPRETING THROUGH?

■

SHAKESPEARE & CO., N.Y.C.

IS THERE ANYTHING NATURAL ABOUT AN
URBAN ENVIRONMENT?

DOG SHIT AND GARBAGE.

■

HUDSON STREET PAPERS, N.Y.C.

HOW DO YOU LOVINGLY HOUSEBREAK
A PROBLEM DOG?

YOU HOLD LOVING THOUGHTS AS YOU SMACK IT FIRMLY

BUT GENTLY EVERY TIME IT PIDDLES OR POOPS OFF PAPER.

THIS MIGHT BE HARD FOR A WOMAN, SINCE FIRMNESS AND

LOVE ARE NOT THE COMBO WOMAN WORKS IN.

STAGHORN, N.Y.C.

WHY DOES EVERY SECOND NEW YORKER TALK TO HIMSELF ON THE STREET?

I'VE BEEN PONDERING THIS MYSELF. EVEN WELL-DRESSED, MONEYED FOLKS WALK AROUND THE CITY STREETS CARRYING ON A DIALOGUE WITH THEMSELVES OUT LOUD. NEW YORK IS A LONELY PLACE AND HAS ALWAYS SEEMED TO ME THE BIRTH AREA OF NEUROSIS. THESE STREET TALKERS ARE SO INVOLVED IN THEIR OWN INNER BABBLE THAT THEY DON'T KNOW THEY'RE SPEAKING IT, I THINK, NOR DO MANY OF THEM HAVE ANYONE TO CONVERSE WITH. SINCE NO VETERAN NEW YORKER IS GOING TO LET *ANYTHING* STOP THEM, THEY GET THEIR CONVERSATION NEEDS MET THE BEST WAY THEY CAN. ONE MORNING I SAW A LOVELY YOUNG WOMAN, LOOKING IN EVERY RESPECT NOT ONLY SANE BUT INTELLIGENT, WALKING DOWN EIGHTEENTH STREET AND BROADWAY WITH HER EYES CLOSED, TALKING TO HERSELF. WAS THAT WALKING MEDITATION OR WALKING INSANITY? MAYBE THE NEXT TIME YOU SEE SOMEONE TALKING TO HIMSELF, YOU'LL ANSWER HIM— PROVIDE A LITTLE INSTANT SHOCK TREATMENT.

GALISTEO NEWS, SANTA FE, N.M.

WHY DO WE HAVE A DRUG PROBLEM?

BECAUSE WE HAVE

A LIFE PROBLEM

A LOVE PROBLEM

AN ALIGNMENT PROBLEM

A VALUE PROBLEM

A POWER PROBLEM

A SEX PROBLEM

A FRUSTRATION PROBLEM

A LIFE-AS-A-PILE-OF-SHIT PROBLEM.

■

THE VILLAGE VOICE, N.Y.C.

WHY AM I GAY, AND HOW CAN I CURE IT?

YOU'RE GAY BECAUSE YOUR SOUL IS MAKING A TRANSI-
TION FROM MALE TO FEMALE (OR VICE VERSA). YOU'LL
CURE IT WHEN YOU'VE MADE THE ADJUSTMENT, WHICH
WILL PROBABLY BE IN THE NEXT LIFE. IF IT'S IN THIS LIFE,
YOUR "CURE" WILL BE ACCEPTANCE.

STAGHORN, N.Y.C.

WILL I SPEND THE REST OF MY LIFE BEING FAT?
(Asked by a woman)

IF YOU'RE OVER FORTY, PROBABLY. BUT YOU CAN MAKE YOUR *THINKING* LEANER, BY CONSIDERING NOT THAT YOU ARE *FAT* BUT ZAFTIG, AMPLE, FULL MOTHER. YOU'VE COME INTO YOUR TIME TO ENJOY *WHO* YOU ARE WITHOUT HAVING TO BE GORGEOUS TO CATCH THE MATE OF YOUR LIFE, SO HAVE A GOOD TIME WITH IT! IT IS THE NATURE OF WOMAN TO HAVE MORE FAT TISSUE IN HER SYSTEM, AND FROM THE BEGINNING OF HUMAN LIFE, WOMEN HAVE, AFTER CHILDBIRTH, BEEN DEPICTED AS ROUND AND AMPLE. WHY FIGHT IT? PROMOTE ITS VIRTUES, ESPECIALLY IN YOUR OWN MIND.

■

GALISTEO NEWS, SANTA FE, N.M.

WHY DO SOME PEOPLE LIKE TO BE ALONE?

THERE'S NO MORE CONGENIAL COMPANY THAN ONE'S SELF.

GALISTEO NEWS, SANTA FE, N.M.

WHY DOES THE WHITE MAN NOT CHERISH THE EARTH, AS THE INDIAN DOES?

THE WHITE MAN LIKES TO CREATE HIS OWN WORLD; THE INDIAN LIKES TO CHERISH THE WORLD CREATION HAS MADE FOR HIM.

∎

THE VILLAGE VOICE, N.Y.C.

IS ALL FASHION A POSE?

FASHION AT THE ROOT IS *FORM*, AND *POSE* AT THE ROOT IS A PAUSE. PERHAPS, THEN, ALL FASHION THAT IS DETERMINED BY ANYONE BUT ONE'S SELF IS A PAUSE IN THE DEVELOPMENT OF ONE'S TRUE FORM. ASIDE FROM THAT ESOTERIC CONTEMPLATION, FASHION DOES HELP US STRIKE A PARTICULAR POSE; EVEN MORE, IT ARMORS US TO WITHSTAND THE BLOWS OF THOSE STRIVING TO BECOME INTIMATE WITH WHO WE REALLY ARE.

∎

THE LIVING BATCH BOOKSTORE, ALBUQUERQUE, N.M.

WRITE ABOUT PREVENTING NUCLEAR WAR.

PRAY. STOP FIGHTING AT HOME. STOP FIGHTING IN YOUR HEAD WITH THOSE WHOSE PERSONALITY TRAITS PISS YOU OFF. IMAGINE THE WORLD AT PEACE. NUCLEAR WAR STARTS AT HOME.

GALISTEO NEWS, SANTA FE, N.M.

WHY CAN'T WHITE PEOPLE DANCE?
(ESPECIALLY MEN.)

BOTH COLOR AND RHYTHM ARE BLEACHED OUT OF MOST WHITE FOLK, ESPECIALLY MEN: UNLESS THEY'RE ARTISTS AND BOHEMIANS OR, SOMETIMES, CRIMINALS.

THE GAMUT, SANTA FE, N.M.

IS MADNESS VALID IN TODAY'S SOCIETY?

NOT ONLY VALID BUT UTTERLY NECESSARY. AS ABOVE, SO BELOW: THE SOCIETY IS MAD; TO DEAL WITH IT, *WE MUST BE*.

THE GAMUT, SANTA FE, N.M.

HOW CAN BLACKS AND JEWS RESOLVE
THEIR CONFLICTS?

BY FORGETTING THEY'RE JEWS OR BLACKS.

THE VILLAGE VOICE, N.Y.C.

**MY GIRLFRIEND, FROM CHICAGO, WANTS TO
KNOW WHY WAITERS IN NEW YORK DON'T
AUTOMATICALLY BRING YOU MUSTARD WHEN
THEY BRING YOU KETCHUP TO GO WITH
YOUR HAMBURGER. THEY DO
IN THE MIDWEST.**

FOR THE SAME REASON THEY DON'T BRING YOU MAYON-
NAISE, AS THEY DO IN CALIFORNIA. FOR NEW YORKERS,
ONLY NEW YORK WAYS EXIST: ANYONE FROM ANYWHERE
ELSE IN AMERICA HAS NO TASTE AT ALL.

■

THE GAMUT, SANTA FE, N.M.

WHY SHOULD WE BE IN SANTA FE?

FOR CENTERING,
FOR REST AND RECUPERATION.
FOR OPENING THE MIND TO WIDER VISION AND THE
SPECIAL, GOLDEN LIGHT OF SANTA FE. EVERY BIG-CITY
DWELLER NEEDS TO SPEND TIME IN SANTA FE. SANTA FE,
INDEED ALL OF NORTHERN NEW MEXICO, IS A
SANATORIUM FOR CITY FOLK.

THE GAMUT, SANTA FE, N.M.

WHAT SHOULD I BUY TO TAKE HOME TO MY PARENTS IN DALLAS? I DON'T HAVE MUCH MONEY.

DON'T BUY, THEN. GO HIKING, WALK THE HILLS AND ARROYOS. PICK UP THE BEAUTIFUL STONES, THE SKELETONS OF CHOLLA (PRONOUNCED "CHOYA") CACTUS, EXQUISITELY CRISSCROSSED NATURAL SCULPTURE. YOU MAY EVEN FIND SOME SNAKE VERTEBRAE, BLEACHED PURE WHITE BY THE SUN. BRING THESE TO YOUR PARENTS AS A TRUE GIFT OF SANTA FE AND YOUR OWN EFFORT; OR USE YOUR NATURE FINDINGS TO *CREATE* A GIFT. YOU WILL HAVE ENJOYED YOURSELF, SEEN THE SIGHTS, SAVED MONEY, AND LEARNED SOMETHING ABOUT TRUE GIVING.

THE GAMUT, SANTA FE, N.M.

SINCE I CAME TO THE UNITED STATES, I NOTICED THAT IN YOUNG PEOPLE, A TOPIC FOR CONVERSATION IS NOTHING RELATED WITH POLITICS OR PHILOSOPHY OR RELIGION OR OTHER IMPORTANT SUBJECTS. I HAVE BEEN LISTENING TO THE YOUNG PEOPLE TALK ABOUT HOW THEY EAT THE "OREOS" COOKIES THAT DAY. ARE THERE IN THOSE COOKIES SOMETHING SPECIAL THAT I'M MISSING, OR IS THIS TOPIC OF CONVERSATION PART OF THE AMERICAN FOLKLORE?

AMERICANS CONSUME ALL THINGS SENSUAL AND VERY LITTLE THAT IS PHILOSOPHICAL OR SERIOUSLY SOCIAL. IN BOTH FOODSTUFF AND MINDSTUFF, WE AMERICANS FEED ON THESE THINGS YOU HEAR ABOUT CALLED OREO COOKIES: TOO-SWEET VANILLA CREME SANDWICHED BETWEEN TOO-SWEET MAKE-BELIEVE CHOCOLATE COOKIES. FOR MORE FOLKLORE OF THE SURFACE-SURFING AMERICAN, WATCH OUR TELEVISION FOR A MONTH. YOU'LL BE AMAZED THAT AMERICANS CAN THINK AT ALL!

■

GALISTEO NEWS, SANTA FE, N.M.

WHEN DO WE STOP ASKING QUESTIONS? LIFE IS SIMPLE.

BUT CIVILIZATION IS NOT!

HUDSON STREET PAPERS, N.Y.C.

HOW CAN I AVOID HELPING EVERY SCHMUCK WHO LEAVES A BLEEDING-HEART NOTE ON THE STREET?

THINK CREATIVELY, CHANGE THE RULE: REALIZE YOU'RE HELPING BY SHOWING YOUR RESPECT FOR SELF-SUFFICIENCY. BLESS THE SCHMUCK AND WALK ON.

■

GALISTEO NEWS, SANTA FE, N.M.

WHY ARE THERE SO MANY "FAKE" PEOPLE IN THE WORLD?

TO BE FAKE IS TO BE CIVILIZED, AND WE ARE AT THE DEATH-DEALING HEIGHT OF CIVILIZATION. FAKERY, TOO, IS A GOOD PROTECTIVE DEVICE, AN EFFICIENT ARMORING AGAINST BOTH ONE'S OWN INSIGHT AND THE REST OF HUMANITY'S "FAKE" ONSLAUGHT. "FAKE" IS TOUTED AS THE THING TO BE. WEAR SPIKE HEELS, PAINT YOUR LIPS CHERRY RED, YOUR EYELIDS COBALT BLUE, KNOT YOUR NECK WITH THAT TIE, POLISH THOSE SHOES, DON'T FART IN PUBLIC, NEVER, NEVER STRAY BEYOND THE CODE OF PROPER BEHAVIOR, STRIVE TO BE A SAINT, LIVE AS IF YOU WERE, MOUTH THE WORDS OF SEXUAL PROPRIETY, I PRAY YOU, BUT JERK OFF IN PRIVATE: THESE ARE THE BEHAVIORS SOCIETY DECREES. BREAK AWAY: DO YOUR SHARE TO SHAKE FAKERY.

THE GAMUT, SANTA FE, N.M.

WHERE ARE THE POOR PEOPLE IN SANTA FE? WILL I BE WAITED ON IN SHOPS IF I DO NOT WEAR DESIGNER CLOTHES?
—"A Poor Student"

THE POOR PEOPLE HAVE BEEN TUCKED AWAY IN THE BARRIOS OUTSIDE THE MAIN AND RICH PART OF SANTA FE. NOW, OF COURSE, THOSE BARRIOS ARE BEING TAKEN OVER BY THE WEALTHY TOO, REMODELED INTO HOTSY-TOTSY BUT QUAINT ADOBE HACIENDAS FOR THE WEALTHY REFUGEES FROM BIG CITIES WHO LONG TO BECOME ADOBE ARISTOCRATS. YES, YOU'LL BE WAITED ON IN SANTA FE STORES WITHOUT HAVING TO WEAR DESIGNER CLOTHES. SANTA FE IS A TOWN OF WEALTHY AND POOR ECCENTRICS. WE NEVER KNOW WHETHER YOU'RE HIDING YOUR BUCKS IN THE BACKPACK OR HAVE SPENT ALL YOUR MONEY ON DESIGNER CLOTHES.

B. DALTON, N.Y.C.

TOPIC SUGGESTION: LUNCH HOUR

THE "HOUR" NEEDS TO BE PLURAL, A TWO-HOUR "SIESTA" SO THAT THERE IS TIME TO REFRESH ONESELF FROM THE OFFICE ROUTINE—TIME NOT ONLY TO EAT A LOVELY LUNCH BUT TO WALK, TO SHOP, TO RELAX. EXECUTIVES TAKE TWO-HOUR LUNCHES; WHY DON'T THE REST OF THE CREW? I HOPE EMPLOYERS REALIZE BY NOW THAT THE BETTER THE WORKER IS TREATED, THE BETTER THE WORKER WORKS.

■

THE GAMUT, SANTA FE, N.M.

WHY ARE THE RICH SO RUDE?

THEY CAN AFFORD TO BE.

CARDS & SUCH, FOREST HILLS, N.Y.

HOW DO YOU ACCOUNT FOR THE LACK OF POLITENESS AND CONSIDERATION BETWEEN YOUNG AND OLD?

THE OLD HAVE MADE NO ATTEMPT TO UNDERSTAND AND RESPECT THE VIEWS OF THE YOUNG, AND SO THE YOUNG RETURN THE INSULT.

■

VERY SPECIAL ARTS, ALBUQUERQUE, N.M.

WHAT CAN I DO TO CONTRIBUTE TO PEACE, STABILITY, AND OPENNESS IN THE WORLD?

MANIFEST ALL THIS YOURSELF, IN YOUR OWN EVERY MOMENT LIVING.

■

GALISTEO NEWS, SANTA FE, N.M.

WHY DO OTHERWISE NORMAL, NON-ILL PEOPLE COUGH AS IF THEY WERE DYING OF TB BETWEEN MOVEMENTS OF SYMPHONIES DURING CONCERTS?

BECAUSE THE ONLY PHYSICAL MOVEMENT POSSIBLE DUR-ING SYMPHONIES IS THAT WHICH YOU CAN STEAL BETWEEN MUSICAL MOVEMENTS: CONCERT-WATCHING IS RATHER A CONSTIPATED EVENT. MUSIC IS TO DANCE TO, OR TO LISTEN TO WHILE YOU'RE SPRAWLED COMFY AND

COZY IN YOUR EASY CHAIR. TECHNOLOGY HAS MADE THE CONCERT HALL OBSOLETE UNLESS IT'S IN YOUR LIVING ROOM, BUT THE PATRICIAN HOI POLLOI REFUSE TO UNDERSTAND THAT, AND STILL SIT STIFF-SHIRTED IN STRAIGHT CHAIRS AND STALE-AIR ROOMS. THE FACT THAT ALL THESE POOR, BORED, STRUCTURED FOLKS CAN MAN-AGE TO DO IS COUGH VIOLENTLY ATTESTS TO THE CON-STRICTION THEY'VE ALLOWED IN THEIR LIVES. WHY DON'T THEY GET UP AND SCREAM, OR STAND UP AND STRETCH, OR DO A SMALL JIG?

■

THE VILLAGE VOICE, N.Y.C.

WHAT IS THE "DINK, DINK, DINK" YOU HEAR IN DEPARTMENT STORES?

EVERY "DINK" IS A CASH TRANSACTION. THIS IS THE STORE'S INSTANT TALLY. THE "DINKING" HAS A LITTLE SUB-LIMINAL TWIST TO IT, FOR IT INCREASES THE SHOPPER'S HUNGER TO CONSUME MORE, MORE, MORE.

■

HUDSON STREET PAPERS, N.Y.C.

WHY SHOULD A NICE STORE LIKE THIS SELL PLASTIC CHOCOLATES?

TO HEIGHTEN YOUR AWARENESS!

B. DALTON, N.Y.C.

WHAT IS NEW YORK?

NEW YORK IS THE STILETTO CITY OF SHIVA, THE DESTROYER OF ILLUSIONS. IT WILL SHAFT YOU AND DEMAND THAT YOU LIVE AFTER BEING SHAFTED, AND SUC-CEED *BECAUSE* OF THE SHAFT. NEW YORK IS THE TOUGH-ENER OF PERSONALITY, THE TEACHER OF THE HARD WAY TO GO, THE POSTGRADUATE COURSE IN SUCCESS. NEW YORK IS AMERICA'S CAPITAL OF SENSUOUSNESS, IF NOT GLUTTONY. ALL SENSUAL DELIGHTS, FROM GOURMET EAT-ING TO SWINGING SEX IN A NIGHTCLUB, ARE AVAILABLE IN NEW YORK. NEW YORK IS WHERE THE GOLD FLAGS OF MONEY FLY. NEW YORK IS WHERE THE MOST NEUROTIC PEOPLE IN THE LAND GROW. NEW YORK IS, FOR ALL THIS, GLORIOUSLY, TOTALLY *ALIVE!*

COLLEGE OF SANTA FE, SANTA FE, N.M.

WHY DO PEOPLE FOLLOW
THE GRATEFUL DEAD?

THE GRATEFUL DEAD ARE THE "LEADERS" OF A "CLUB," THE HEADSTONE (DOUBLE MEANING INTENDED) FOR UNDERGROUND-CULTURE "JOINERS." A GREAT MANY OF THE "DEAD" FOLLOWERS ARE FROM "OUTLAW BIKER" CLUBS—EX-MEMBERS AND CURRENT MEMBERS, THEIR "OL' LADIES" AND KIN, OF SUCH INFAMOUS BANDS OF MODERN PIRATES AS HELL'S ANGELS, BANDIDOS, VAGOS, DEVIL'S DISCIPLES, TO NAME A FEW. BESIDE THESE RAW-PASSION GROUPIES ARE THE COMMUNE-JOINERS OF THE SIXTIES AND THEIR KIN. WHAT MAKES A LIFE OF FOLLOWING THE "DEAD" SO ATTRACTIVE? THE FLUIDITY, THE CONTINUA-TION OF THE SIXTIES' TUNE-IN, DROP-OUT PHENOMENA. THOSE WITH THE "DEAD" AS THEIR GYPSY-CARAVAN LEAD-ERS CAN GO THROUGH LIFE HAPPILY TRIPPING TO MUSIC AND EUPHORICS, DANCING TO THE UNDULATING RHYTHMS OF THEIR MUSICAL MASTERS WHILE MAKING A LIVING. IT'S NOT MY BOWL OF TEA, BUT SOUNDS LIKE IT BEATS THE NINE-TO-FIVE FLUORESCENT-LIGHT ROUTINE, YES?

GALISTEO NEWS, SANTA FE, N.M.

PLEASE WRITE ABOUT AIDS.

SUCH PAIN. SUCH UNREADINESS IN ITS HOSTS. SUCH A CALAMITY TO BEAR. IN A RECENT RADIO INTERVIEW, I HEARD AN AIDS PATIENT SPEAK ABOUT A DAY IN THE LIFE WITH AIDS. THE PREGNANT PAUSES BETWEEN HIS STATE-MENTS MADE HIS AGONY FEELABLE TO THE LISTENER. NOW THAT THE DISEASE HAD BROKEN HIM DOWN TO NEEDING INTRAVENOUS FEEDING, HELP FROM A FRIEND TO TAKE A BATH OR A WALK, HE REALIZED THE VALUE OF THESE ONCE TAKEN-FOR-GRANTED SIMPLE PLEASURES OF LIFE. NOW HE WAS ASKING HIMSELF QUESTIONS HE NEVER THOUGHT HE'D ASK: "SHOULD I PERHAPS NOT HAVE BEEN SO PROMISCUOUS? WHAT IF I'D BEEN STRAIGHT?" HE WAS QUESTIONING THE VERY TENETS HE'D LIVED BY, AND THIS WAS IN ITSELF EXCRUCIATING FOR HIM; BUT COUPLED WITH THE PHYSICAL PAIN OF HIS CONDITION . . . HE SPOKE OF HOW UNREADY FOR DEATH HE WAS, HOW MUCH RAGE HE FELT, THOUGH HE COULD PUT IT ON NO ONE AND NOTHING. I CAME AWAY FROM THAT INTERVIEW WITH A BETTER UNDERSTANDING OF THE HEROIC LIVES AIDS VIC-TIMS ARE LIVING.

I DON'T KNOW WHY IT HAPPENED, AIDS. I'VE READ REPORTS THAT THE VIRUS WAS LET OUT ACCIDENTALLY IN IMMUNIZATION SHOTS; THAT IT WAS RIGHT-WING GERM WARFARE. WE'LL NOT KNOW FOR A LONG TIME, IF EVER, THE TRUTH OF ITS ORIGIN. CERTAINLY MANY OF THE BATHHOUSE FUN AND GAMES NEEDED TO BE STOPPED— SEX TAKEN TO ITS MOST DISCONNECTED STATE; AND CERTAINLY LIFE CORRECTS ITSELF THROUGH CALAMITY. AIDS IS THE PLAGUE OF THE END OF THE TWENTIETH CENTURY, AND IT'S MARKED ASTROLOGICALLY: WITH PLUTO, THE PLANET OF DEATH AND TRANSFORMATION, IN SCORPIO, THE SIGN OF SEX AND DEATH. WE NEED TO USE THIS PLAGUE TO UNDERSTAND OUR SEXUAL BELIEFS AND PRACTICES, AND OUR ABILITY, OR LACK OF IT, TO HELP EACH OTHER. WE NEED TO OPEN UP TO WHAT DEATH IS AND LEARN HOW WE CAN FACE DEATH WITHOUT FEAR. NO EASY TASK, AND NOT MANY TEACHERS TO GUIDE US— EXCEPT THAT CONSTANT ONE, *EXPERIENCE*.

GALISTEO NEWS, SANTA FE, N.M.

IF YOU'VE VISUALIZED WORLD PEACE, HAVE
YOU DONE ANYTHING ABOUT IT?

PERHAPS YOU'VE MADE A SMALL ENGRAM OF A REMINDER
TO YOURSELF, BUT HOW MUCH YOU'VE *DONE* IS TOLD BY
HOW LONG IT TAKES FOR THE FIRST ANGRY THOUGHT TO
CROSS YOUR MIND, SPITEFUL WORD TO LEAVE YOUR
MOUTH, OR RESENTFUL PUNCH TO FORCE YOUR FIST.

■

GALISTEO NEWS, SANTA FE, N.M.

WHAT TREND CAN ONE FOLLOW TO BE A
STEP AHEAD?

YOUR VERY OWN AND NO ONE ELSE'S.

■

GALISTEO NEWS, SANTA FE, N.M.

WHAT DO YOU DO WHEN EVERYTHING SHITS
ON YOU AND YOU LOOK TO THE DEEPEST
YOU AND CAN FIND NO REASON FOR IT?
—"Pissed Off"

DEAR PISSED OFF:
THE DAY HAS NOT COME WHEN, UPON LOOKING TO THE
DEEPEST ME, I CANNOT FIND A REASON, A CAUSE OF MY
OWN MAKING, FOR THE SHIT THAT IS COMING DOWN
UPON ME AT THE TIME. THIS DOESN'T MEAN THERE IS NO

CAUSE, NO BLAME TO BE CAST ON OUTER CIRCUM-
STANCES. IT SIMPLY MEANS: IF YOU'RE IN THE PLACE
WHERE THE TORNADO IS WHIRLING, YOU'VE GOT TO
QUESTION HOW YOU GOT THERE AND WHY YOU DIDN'T
CHECK UP ON WEATHER CONDITIONS.

■

GALISTEO NEWS, SANTA FE, N.M.

A WORD ON COYOTE ART, PLEASE;
THE CORRELATION OF AFFLUENCE TO
TASTELESSNESS;
METAPHYSICAL ASPECTS OF OPULENCE;
THE RELATIONSHIP OF FAIRER SKIN COLORS
TO OBESITY IN SANTA FE.
Many thanks, The Wave

COYOTE ART: THE AD-NAUSEAMNESS OF COYOTE ART FINDS
ITS ROOTS IN A SWEET THING MADE CLOYING. LIKE
CHRIST'S SHROUD, THE GURU'S ROBES, THE ROCK STAR'S
JACKET, THE MOVIE QUEEN'S RESOLD NIGHTIE: A PIECE OF
THE GREAT PIE HOLDS PROMISE OF BRINGING US CLOSER
TO OUR IDEAL IDOL. SANTA FE HAS ITSELF BECOME A COY-
OTE, SELLING ITSELF DOWN THE CACTUS-KITSCH ARROYO.
REDUNDANT ON T-SHIRTS, EARRINGS, WOOD CARVINGS,
IN EVERY STORE WINDOW ON THE BLOCK, THE COYOTE
HAS BECOME THE BITCH OF BUSINESS. BUT OUR BUSINESS
IN SANTA FE IS TO GIVE OUTLANDERS A TASTE OF THE

MAGICAL, STRANGE SOUTHWEST. WE WOULD NOT BE ABLE TO AFFORD THIS HIDEAWAY LIVING IF WE DIDN'T ATTRACT EYE AND PURSE WITH CLOYING COYOTE AND CACTUS ART. ALL BUSINESS IS PROSTITUTION, ALL BUSINESS THAT CAUSES WORK TO BE DONE NOT FOR LOVE OF THE WORK BUT FOR WHAT WE CAN GET FOR DOING IT.

THE CORRELATION OF AFFLUENCE TO TASTELESSNESS IS NOT NECESSARILY THERE. I HAVE OBSERVED GREAT TASTE IN THE AFFLUENT. BUT BAD TASTE IS STILL TASTE. THE GOOD TASTE OF PORK RINDS VS. THAT OF BEEF WELLINGTON IS ALL IN THE MIND OF THE EXPERIENCER.

THE RELATIONSHIP OF FAIRER SKIN COLORS TO OBESITY IN SANTA FE IS NO STRONGER THAN IS THE RELATIONSHIP OF OBESITY AND AMERICA. IN FACT, I FIND OBESITY MORE RELATIVE TO THE NATIVE AMERICAN AND THE CHICANO IN SANTA FE AND TO WOMEN IN GENERAL. TO THE LATTER I WILL SPEAK: THE MOAT OF OBESITY KEEPS THE DEMONS AWAY, THE FEARED INVOLVEMENT WITH WHAT THE MOATED-SHE SENSES WILL CAUSE MORE PAIN THAN THE MOAT CAUSES AND GIVE LESS PLEASURE FOR MORE WORK THAN DOES THE FOOD THAT BUILDS THE MOAT.

METAPHYSICAL ASPECTS OF OPULENCE: MAKING HEAVEN IN HELL TAKES A LOT OF GLITTER AND GOLD!

GALISTEO NEWS, SANTA FE, N.M.

DO YOU HAVE ANY TIPS FOR BETTER LIVING DURING THE APOCALYPSE?

HELP OR HIDE.

■

GALISTEO NEWS, SANTA FE, N.M.

I AM SLOWLY LOSING FRIENDS AND SLOWLY LOSING MY HAPPINESS. WHAT CAN I DO?

OBSERVE, BE AWARE OF HOW AND WHY THIS HAPPENS, OF YOUR OWN RESPONSIBILITY IN THE ENDING, AND OF WHERE YOUR RESPONSIBILITY STOPS AND THE FRIEND'S STARTS. SEEK THE SYMBOLS THAT CAN IMPART UNDER-STANDING, AND THE WISDOMS. OLD INFLUENCES ARE BEING SHED, WITHIN AND WITHOUT YOU. THIS IS A TIME TO BECOME YOUR OWN BEST FRIEND AND GUIDE. IF THIS LOSING IS CAUSED BY PHYSICAL DEATH, MAKE DEATH YOUR TEACHER AND RE-LEASOR.

■

THE GAMUT, SANTA FE, N.M.

WHY DO PEOPLE TRY TO CHANGE EACH OTHER?

BECAUSE IT'S EASIER THAN CHANGING THEMSELVES.

GALISTEO NEWS, SANTA FE, N.M.

SOMETIMES JUST RELAXING IS WHAT I ENJOY. AND WATCHING THE WONDROUS SUNSETS, WITH THE WIND BLOWING, IS EVEN NICER. DOES THIS SEEM LIKE A STRANGE WAY TO ENJOY LIFE? HMMM?

IN SOCIETAL TERMS, YES. IN HUMAN TERMS, THIS IS ONE OF THE MAJOR EVENTS WE INCARNATED FOR.

■

GALISTEO NEWS, SANTA FE, N.M.

HOW DID FOOLS COME TO POWER? IS THERE ANY TURNING BACK?

FOOLS CAME TO POWER BECAUSE THE OTHER HUMANS DIDN'T WANT TO BE BOTHERED WITH ANYTHING BUT THEIR OWN SURVIVAL. NO TURNING BACK, BUT NO NEED TO, EITHER: THE LIGHT AT THE END OF THE TUNNEL IS GETTING NEARER. WHEN WE EMERGE INTO THE NEW WORLD *THIS* TIME, WE WILL HAVE QUANTUM-LEAPED OUT OF THE FOLLY OF LETTING GEORGE DO IT, INTO THE JOY OF INDIVIDUAL RESPONSIBILITY.

GALISTEO NEWS, SANTA FE, N.M.

WERE YOU EVER SPANKED AS A CHILD? DO YOU THINK IT WAS EFFECTIVE?

YES, I WAS SPANKED, AND YES, IT WAS EFFECTIVE, THOUGH NOT FOR MY PARENTS' PURPOSES. IT INSTILLED REBELLION IN ME AND DEVELOPED LATER INTO AN UNDERSTANDING THAT PUNISHMENT SERVES NO PURPOSE BUT THAT OF REBELLION AND THE DAMPENING OF THE WIELDER'S FRUSTRATION.

■

GALISTEO NEWS, SANTA FE, N.M.

DEAR GEORGELLE: I HAVE GREAT COMPASSION FOR THE ACCOUNT OF YOUR LIFE. AS YOU COULD HAVE BEEN A DRUNKARD, BUM, JUNKIE, OR WORSE BUT TURNED OUT TO BE A SUCCESSFUL HUMAN BEING, DO YOU HAVE SOME INSIGHT/ SUGGESTIONS FOR THE REST OF US WHO WERE SIMILARLY ABUSED?

RELEASE THE PAIN. FIND YOUR VALUE THROUGH *HOW* YOU LIVE AND IN THE WORK THAT YOU DO. THIS WORK NEEDS TO UTILIZE YOUR ABUSE-GAINED COMPASSION AND BE A WORK OF THE HEART, NOT JUST A *JOB* JOB. KEEP TO WHAT INTERESTS YOU, DO ONLY WHAT INTERESTS YOU, FOR INTEREST IS THE GREAT LIFESAVER. FIND YOUR OWN RIT-UAL FOR CONNECTING WITH THE FIELD OF LIFE THAT IS BEYOND, SURROUNDING, AND WITHIN YOU.

THE VILLAGE VOICE, N.Y.C.

I HEAR VENICE, CALIFORNIA, IS SORT OF FORTY-SECOND-STREET-AND-THE-VILLAGE-GO-TO-THE-BEACH. THIS SOUNDS INTERESTING. IS IT TRUE? CAN YOU TELL US ABOUT IT? SHOULD WE GO?

WHEN I LIVED THERE, I ALWAYS THOUGHT OF VENICE AS AN OUTDOOR SANATORIUM BECAUSE IT'S THE LAST EDGE FOR THE STREET PEOPLE, AND IT'S EASY LIVING TOO. THE STREET PEOPLE LIVE IN THE MANY PAGODAS THAT GRACE OCEANFRONT WALK, TUCKING THEIR GARBAGE-PICKED CLOTHES INTO THE PAGODA RAFTERS DURING THE DAY TO RESERVE THEIR TERRITORY FOR THE NIGHT. THERE ARE OCEANFRONT MINSTRELS WHO PLAY GUITAR AND SING FOR COINS THROWN INTO A HAT. THE MOST FAMOUS OF THESE IS REMEMBERED BY EVERYONE WHO HAS ENCOUNTERED HIM, THE TURBANED TROUBADOUR WHO ROLLERSKATES UP AND DOWN THE BOARDWALK WITH BATTERY PACK AND ELECTRIC GUITAR, SERENADING STROLLERS WITH IMPASSIONED POLITICAL DIATRIBES. ON WEEKENDS, THE BOARDWALK IS LIKE A FELLINI FILM, WITH MOVIE STARS AND PUNKS, CRAZIES AND MUSCLE GIRLS, CROWDING THE WALK TO GAZE AT THE BAZAAR, AND OFTEN BIZARRE, GOODS BEING SOLD ON THE WALKWAY. IT'S A GREAT PIECE OF ENTERTAINMENT. YES, YOU SHOULD GO THERE FOR A WEEKEND, SIT IN ONE OF THE OCEANFRONT CAFÉS AND SIP CAPPUCCINO WHILE YOU WATCH LIFE OUTDO FELLINI.

IS THERE ANY VIRTUE IN WINE?

THERE'S MUCH VIRTUE IN WINE, MORE THAN IN ANY OTHER LIQUOR. WINE IS THE OLDEST EUPHORIC IN HUMANKIND'S HISTORY. EVEN THE ANCIENT CHINESE (IN ABOUT 125 B.C.) WERE VINTNERS. GREAT CARE HAS ALWAYS BEEN TAKEN IN PREPARING THE SOIL FOR THE GRAPES, AND IN AGING AND FERMENTING THE JUICE. RECENTLY THIS STORY ABOUT HOW WINE WAS DISCOVERED CAME MY WAY: THERE WAS A KING WHO LOVED GRAPE JUICE, AND HE KEPT A CELLAR FILLED WITH BARRELS OF IT. ONE DAY, HE WENT TO ONE OF THE BARRELS THAT HAD BEEN THERE A LONG TIME, DRANK, BUT SPIT IT OUT: IT WAS NOT THE SWEET JUICE HE WAS USED TO, BUT BITTER, FOR IT HAD FERMENTED. NOT KNOWING ANY BETTER, THE KING CALLED IT POISON AND LEFT IT IN HIS CELLARS FOR SUCH WARLIKE USE. SOON AFTER, HE BEGAN TO PLAY AROUND WITH WOMEN, AND HIS WIFE FELL OUT OF FAVOR. SO DISTRAUGHT WAS SHE THAT SHE WENT IMMEDIATELY TO THE CELLAR TO POISON HERSELF WITH THE NEWFOUND VENOMOUS LIQUID. MUCH TO HER SURPRISE, SHE DIDN'T DIE, BUT THE MORE SHE DRANK, THE HAPPIER SHE BECAME. HAVING DISCOVERED THE WONDERS OF THIS ELIXIR, SHE STASHED SOME IN HER BEDROOM, AND EVERY NIGHT, SHE'D DRINK A GLASS BEFORE DINNER. THIS MADE

HER SO GAY AND SENSUOUS THAT SHE WON BACK HER HUSBAND'S FAVORS. OF COURSE, THE KING DISCOVERED HER SECRET, AND THEREUPON HAD A GLASS OR FOUR HIMSELF. THUS WAS WINE DISCOVERED. IT ISN'T THAT WINE ISN'T VIRTUOUS. IT'S THAT ABUSE SOILS ITS VIRTUE.

THE GAMUT, SANTA FE, N.M.

PLEASE WRITE ABOUT HAVING TO LOOK AND FOLLOW ADULTS' BORING IDEAS.
(Asked by a nine-year-old)

YES, IT'S A DRAG TO BE A NEW-MINDED SOUL BORN INTO A FAMILY OF UNPROGRESSIVE PERSONALITIES. YOU JUST HAVE TO GRIN AND BEAR IT UNTIL YOU'RE OLD ENOUGH TO STRIKE OUT ON YOUR OWN. AND THERE'S NO NEED TO "BUY" THEIR IDEAS; BUT YOU MIGHT LET THESE IDEAS ENTERTAIN YOU, APPROACH THEM AS A STUDY OF THE PERSONALITIES OF THE ADULTS, IN AN EFFORT TO UNDER-STAND WHAT THEIR DIS-EASE IS AND HOW TO ENSURE THAT YOU NEVER CONTRACT IT IN *YOUR* MATURITY. PATIENCE AND COMPASSION WILL GET YOU THROUGH CHILDHOOD; AND EVEN THOUGH YOU'RE ONLY NINE, YOU'RE CAPABLE OF BEING MORE TOLERANT THAN ADULTS WITH BORING IDEAS.

VERY SPECIAL ARTS, ALBUQUERQUE, N.M.

WHEN WILL WAR END?
(Asked by an eight-year-old)

WHEN WE HUMANS LEARN TO LIVE LOVING, CREATIVE, COMPASSIONATE EXISTENCES, WAR WILL CEASE. I THINK THIS MAY TAKE A LONG, LONG TIME.

■

STAGHORN, N.Y.C.

WHY ARE ADULTS SO HESITANT OF SAYING THEIR AGE?
(Asked by a ten-year old)

BECAUSE WE LIVE IN A COUNTRY THAT MAKES AGING A DISEASE. ADULTS ARE THEREFORE NOT PROUD OF HAVING PUT IN SO MANY YEARS OF LIVING, NOR ARE THEY APPRECIATIVE OF THE WISDOM THEY'VE GAINED THROUGH IT; INSTEAD, THEY GET CAUGHT UP IN HOW THEY LOOK PHYSICALLY AND IN THE FACT THAT PEOPLE THINK ANYONE OVER THIRTY-FIVE IS OLD. SOME ADULTS, THOUGH, ARE NOT HESITANT ABOUT TELLING THEIR AGE. THESE ARE THE YOUNG AT HEART, WISE IN MIND AND ACCEPTING OF PHYSICAL AGING. YOU NEED TO REMIND ADULTS THAT THEY SHOULD BE PROUD OF LIVING SO LONG AND ASK THEM WHAT THEY'VE LEARNED. THAT WAY, YOU'RE HELPING THEM LOVE THEIR AGE.

GALISTEO NEWS, SANTA FE, N.M

WHY IS SCHOOL SO BORING?
(Asked by an eight-year-old)

SCHOOL *SHOULD* BE BORING: BORING AN OPENING RIGHT
INTO YOUR BRIGHT AND INQUIRING MIND!

■

STAGHORN, N.Y.C.

WHY CAN'T KIDS CHEW GUM IN SCHOOL?

THE ONLY REASON TO MOVE YOUR MOUTH CONTINU-
OUSLY IN SCHOOL IS TO EXPOUND UPON THE SUBJECTS
YOU'VE BEEN STUDYING. BESIDES, WHY DO YOU WANT TO
LOOK LIKE A COW CHEWING HER CUD? IF YOU GET IN THE
GUM-CHEWING HABIT, YOU'LL WIND UP CHEAPENING
YOUR IMAGE, LIKE THE CLASSY, MINK-COATED WOMEN OF
MANHATTAN WHOSE NOISY GUM YAPPING MAKES THEM
LOOK LIKE BRONX HOUSEWIVES.

VERY SPECIAL ARTS, ALBUQUERQUE, N.M.

WHY DO I HAVE TO BE A SISTER? AND WHY ARE BIG SISTERS SO MEAN TO LITTLE SISTERS?

YOU'RE JUST LEARNING LESSONS IN RELATING AND POWER. SISTERS ARE TO TEACH US EARLY ON THAT WE HAVE TO TOLERATE FOLKS WHO ARE *REALLY* A DRAG OR BEHAVIOR THAT DOESN'T MAKE US JUMP FOR JOY. AS TO BIG SISTERS BEING MEAN TO LITTLE ONES, IT'S A PROBLEM WITH POWER THAT YOU WILL BOTH ENCOUNTER AS YOU GO ON THROUGH LIFE. THE BIG SISTER HAS TO LEARN TO TEMPER HER POWER POSITION WITH COMPASSION, AND THE LITTLE SISTER HAS TO LEARN NOT TO BUCKLE UNDER JUST BECAUSE BIG SISTER MAKES HER TREMBLE: LITTLE SISTERS HAVE TO LEARN HOW TO STAND UP FOR THEMSELVES.

■

VERY SPECIAL ARTS, ALBUQUERQUE, N.M.

WHY DO PEOPLE HAVE FRECKLES?

FRECKLES ARE A REMINDER THAT THERE'S A LITTLE BROWN EVEN IN THE WHITEST OF US.

VERY SPECIAL ARTS, ALBUQUERQUE, N.M.

WHY DOES MY DAD DRINK?

BECAUSE HE HAS A HARD TIME HANDLING LIFE, HIMSELF, AND THE WORLD AROUND HIM.

■

SHAKESPEARE & CO., N.Y.C.

WHERE DID BOOKSTORES BEGIN?
(Asked by a five-year old)

BOOKSTORES BEGAN IN EUROPE IN THE FIFTEENTH CEN-TURY, AFTER THE INVENTION OF THE PRINTING PRESS. SINCE *PUBLISHERS* OF THE BOOKS THAT WERE TURNED OUT BY THIS NEW PRESS BEGAN TO BLOSSOM IN 1583 IN HOLLAND, IT SEEMS REASONABLE TO PLACE THE FIRST BOOKSTORE IN HOLLAND, IN THE LATE 1500'S–EARLY 1600'S. IN ANCIENT TIMES, BEFORE THE PRINTING PRESS, BOOKS WERE PUT TOGETHER IN LARGE PACKAGES THAT COULD NOT BE CARRIED EASILY, SO HEAVY WERE THEY. THESE LARGE "BOOKS" WERE KEPT IN PALACES OR TEM-PLES, AND PEOPLE CAME *THERE* TO STUDY OR READ, RATHER THAN TAKING THEM HOME. THE PRINTING PRESS MADE LITERATURE AVAILABLE TO EVERYONE, IN THE COM-FORT OF HOME, AND ALLOWED YOUR MOTHER TO BUY FROM A BOOKSTORE WONDERFUL BEDTIME STORIES TO SWEETEN YOUR DREAMS.

GALISTEO NEWS, SANTA FE, N.M.

I CAN LIVE ANYWHERE. WHERE SHOULD I LIVE IN THE U.S.A.? I CAN SPEND $500,000.

IN THAT CASE, THE BEST PLACE, IN MY OPINION, FOR YOU TO LIVE IN THE U.S.A. IS MY SPARE ROOM!

■

HUDSON STREET PAPERS, N.Y.C.

WHY DO I HAVE TO WORK AT SCHOOL WHEN I HAVE NO MOTIVATION TO?

THOUGH SCHOOL NEEDS TO BE EVOKING YOUR MOTIVA-TION TO LEARN (AND CLEARLY ISN'T), IT *IS* TEACHING YOU THROUGH DIRECT EXPERIENCE THAT THERE ARE MANY THINGS IN LIFE THAT YOU WON'T TRULY *WANT* TO DO BUT NEVERTHELESS *MUST* DO IN ORDER TO GET TO THE TASKS THAT *DO* "TURN YOU ON." FURTHER, THOUGH IN MY OPINION TEACHING INSTITUTIONS ARE NOT "UP TO DATE," THEY DO GIVE YOU PRACTICE IN DISCIPLINE, AND DEVELOP WORK AND ORGANIZATION HABITS. YOU'LL NEED THESE ALL THROUGH LIFE, REGARDLESS OF WHAT YOU CHOOSE AS A CAREER. TAKE HEART: IT MUST BE DONE. PRACTICE THE ZEN OF SCHOOLWORK.

HUDSON STREET PAPERS, N.Y.C.

HOW DOES ONE COPE WITH RAMPANT INCOMPETENCE AND SMALL MINDS IN THE BUSINESS WORLD WITHOUT GRINNING AND BEARING IT, OR LEAVING IT?

WHEN YOU SEE THE SMALL MINDS APPROACHING, SAY TO YOURSELF, "ESSENTIAL ENERGY DWELLS WITHIN THAT BEING" AND BOW TO THAT ESSENTIAL ENERGY EVEN AS IT IS BEING OBLITERATED BY THE IDIOCIES OF THE SMALL MIND IT'S ENCASED IN.

■

GALISTEO NEWS, SANTA FE, N.M.

WHAT IS THE PRICE OF PEACE?

FORGIVENESS.

THE VILLAGE VOICE, N.Y.C.

**WHAT DO YOU THINK OF THE PHRASE
"PEACE ON EARTH"? HOW DO YOU THINK WE
CAN MAKE IT "FASHIONABLE" AGAIN?**

WORK ON

PEACE OF MIND.

WHEN YOU GET THAT GOING, WORK ON

PEACE AT HOME.

WHEN THAT IS STRONGLY INSTITUTED, MOVE ON TO

PEACE WHEN YOU DEAL

WITH WAITRONS, SALESPERSONS, AND AD TAKERS;

THEN STRIVE TO MAINTAIN PEACE OF MIND

WHEN TRAVELING DURING RUSH HOUR.

BY THE TIME YOU'VE ACCOMPLISHED THESE PEACE

LESSONS,

YOU'LL KNOW THE CONTINUOUS WORK IT TAKES TO

ACHIEVE PEACE

AND WILL BE SATISFIED THAT YOU ARE ABLE TO BE

A SHINING EXAMPLE IN YOUR PERSONAL LIFE

OF WHAT YOU WOULD LIKE TO SEE IN THE WORLD'S LIFE.

AND YOU'LL UNDERSTAND THAT "PEACE ON EARTH" WILL

TAKE AT LEAST AS

LONG TO ACHIEVE AS DID YOUR OWN PEACE OF MIND.

PEACE BEGINS AT HOME.

LOOKING GLASS BOOKSTORE, PORTLAND, ORE.

WHY DO PRETENTIOUS "ARTISTES" LIVE IN BOOKSTORE WINDOWS JUST WRITING PRETENTIOUS ANSWERS TO MORONIC QUESTIONS? ARE YOU AN AUTHORITY OR SOMETHING?

ARE YOU ANGRY OR SOMETHING? ARTISTS DO THEIR WORK WHEREVER THEY CAN, IN THE HOPE OF SEEDING STILL-SLEEPING MINDS WITH VISIONS OF CREATIVE LIVING AND THINKING. ALL ARTISTS ARE AUTHORITIES ON HOW TO LIVE THE LIFE FANTASTIQUE. ACTUALLY, ALL HUMANS ARE AUTHORS OF THEIR OWN DESTINY, HENCE AUTHORITIES. I'M GLAD YOU QUESTION MY AUTHORITY, AND HOPE YOU TRUST ENOUGH IN YOURS TO KEEP IT GROWING.

■

HUDSON STREET PAPERS, N.Y.C.

WHY IS MY BOSS ALIVE?

SOMEONE HAS TO LEARN PATIENCE AND COMPASSION— OBVIOUSLY YOUR BOSS IS TEACHING YOU A STRONG LESSON!

■

GALISTEO NEWS, SANTA FE, N.M.

WHAT IS THE ESSENCE OF SANTA FE SPIRIT?

FREEDOM.

GALISTEO NEWS, SANTA FE, N.M.

WHY DO MUSICIANS TEND TO BE STRANGE PEOPLE?

THEY SPEAK IN THE LANGUAGE OF THE SPHERES, THEY THINK IN THE PULSATING REALM OF PARTICLES AND WAVES. THEY HEAR ANOTHER RHYTHM THAN DO WE LIN-EAR MORTALS. THEY ARE THE SOUND-HEALERS PLAYING TO HEAL AND BE HEALED OF WORLD WOUNDS.

GALISTEO NEWS, SANTA FE, N.M.

WHAT DOES THE TERM "FUCK YOU" MEAN LITERALLY?

LITERALLY, IT MEANS TO STRIKE, MOVE QUICKLY, PENE-TRATE SOMEONE. THE WORD, AND THE LATTER MEANING, COMES FROM THE GERMANIC VERB *FUCKEN*, WHICH IS, THE DICTIONARY SAYS, BORROWED FROM MIDDLE DUTCH *FOKKEN*, "TO STRIKE, COPULATE WITH." INTERESTING THAT FROM THE EARLIEST USE OF THIS VERB, SEXUAL INTER-COURSE WAS ASSIMILATED WITH THE VIOLENCE OF STRIK-ING. LOOKING FURTHER INTO THE ORIGIN OF THIS WORD "FUCK," THE MEANING GETS WORSE. THE "ROOT OF THE ROOT" IS *PEIG*, "EVIL-MINDED, HOSTILE . . . TREACHEROUS, FALSE, FICKLE . . . ENEMY, FOE . . . FATED TO DIE . . . HOSTIL-ITY, FEUD." SO *NEVER* TELL THOSE YOU LOVE THAT YOU WANT TO FUCK THEM!

GALISTEO NEWS, SANTA FE, N.M.

**WHY CAN THE CURRENT FIRST-PLACE 1989
PRO-AM INTERNATIONAL GAY RODEO
ASSOCIATION DANCE CHAMPION AFFORD TO
SPEND HUNDREDS OF DOLLARS ON
COSTUMES BUT WON'T PART WITH HIS PEE-
STAINED, SKID-MARKED, THREADBARE,
AND TORN UNDERWEAR?
—"Third-Place Winner and Observer
in the Dressing Room"**

DEAR WINNER AND OBSERVER:

THIS DANCE CHAMPION IS IN SHOW BUSINESS TO SHOW
THE FACE HE WANTS TO BE. THIS IS HOW HE IS LEARNING
TO AT LAST LOVE HIS REAL AND INNER FACE ENOUGH TO
CLOAK IT IN SILKEN UNDIES.

■

GALISTEO NEWS, SANTA FE, N.M.

**AS I'M LOSING FRIENDS TO AIDS, WHAT
CONSOLATION CAN I FIND IN LIVING
WITHOUT THEM?**

THERE BUT FOR GRACE, GO YOU. . . .

SO RIDE YOUR TIME LIKE A BANSHEE; IT'S THE MORE INTER-
ESTING ALTERNATIVE TO WEEPING AND WAILING AND
WANING YOUR OWN ENERGIES. GRIEVE AND GO ON.
REMEMBER THEM, FEEL THEM IN THE ETHER, BRING THE
MEMORY OF THEM INTO YOUR JOY. RELEASE. RE-LEASE.

GALISTEO NEWS, SANTA FE, N.M.

IF LIFE IS A BANQUET, WHY ARE SO MANY PEOPLE STARVING TO DEATH?

SOMEONE CORNERED THE BANQUET MARKET AND JACKED THE PRICE UP SO HIGH ONLY A FEW CAN AFFORD THE FEAST.

GALISTEO NEWS, SANTA FE, N.M.

MUST THE MUSIC STOP BECAUSE THE ASSHOLE CONDUCTOR HAD THE AUDACITY TO DIE?

IF IT MUST, WE MAY SEE PART OF THE DESPAIR THAT BECAME A COMPONENT OF THIS CONDUCTOR'S DEATH: A GROUP THAT LEANED ON HIM FOR THE WILL TO MAKE MUSIC. BUT NO, THE MUSIC NEED NOT STOP; IT TAKES A LOT OF LOVE TO KEEP IT GOING, THOUGH.

GALISTEO NEWS, SANTA FE, N.M.

HOW DO WE BEGIN TO TRANSFORM OUR CULTURE? THIS IS A SERIOUS QUESTION.

YOU'RE NOT KIDDING—IT'S A SERIOUS QUESTION. IT BEGINS, THIS TRANSFORMATION OF THE CULTURE, WITH EACH OF US IN THE CULTURE. WITH YOU. WITH ME. WITH YOUR COURAGE IN EXPRESSING AND ACTING ON YOUR VISION OF HOW YOU WANT THE CULTURE TO BE. CORNY, CLICHÉ, OFTEN SAID FOR EONS, BUT TRUE. IN THE NEXT DAY, OR THE NEXT TEN MINUTES, SEE WHETHER OR NOT YOU'RE DOING THIS; AND IF YOU ARE, HOW CONSTANT ARE YOU WITH IT? AND IF YOU'RE NOT, I HOPE YOU'LL START. THE ONLY WAY TO TEACH IS THROUGH YOUR OWN ACTION. IT TAKES A LOT OF COURAGE TO GO AGAINST THE GRAIN.

GALISTEO NEWS, SANTA FE, N.M.

WHAT'S THE DIFFERENCE BETWEEN RED AND GREEN CHILI?

AGE. RED CHILI IS THE DRIED-UP MATRIARCH OF THE GREEN CHILI FAMILY. GREEN CHILIS ARE YOUNG ADULTS, PLUMP WITH DESIRE TO SPICE UP YOUR STEW. RED CHILIS ARE ACTUALLY GREEN CHILIS LEFT TO RIPEN AND DRY ON THE *RISTRA*, OR STRING. RED CHILI HAS AN ABUNDANCE OF VITAMIN A AND GENERALLY BREWS UP TO A COOLER DISH THAN DOES GREEN CHILI. THE ONE EXCEPTION TO THIS IS *CARNE ADOVADA*, PORK MARINATED FOR DAYS IN RED CHILI, NEW MEXICO'S VERSION OF SAUERBRATEN. GREEN CHILI, WHICH IS CHOCK-FULL OF VITAMIN C, CAN BE EATEN NOT ONLY AS A SAUCE AND A STEW BUT, ONCE ROASTED AND PEELED, CAN BE STUFFED WITH CHEESE (*CHILI RELLENOS*) OR BETWEEN TWO PIECES OF BREAD. THE LATTER IS GREAT FOR CLEARING A STUFFY NOSE, ESPE-CIALLY WHEN USING CHILIS FROM HATCH, NEW MEXICO, THE STATE'S HOTTEST VARIETY OF CHILI.

GALISTEO NEWS, SANTA FE, N.M.

DON'T YOU KNOW THAT CABALLEROS WERE, AND STILL ARE, IN THIS TOWN LONG BEFORE HIPPIES, GAYS, FEMINISTS, AND RICH ANGLOS LIKE YOU EVEN KNEW IT EXISTED?! YOUR MISINFORMED, SEXIST, RACIST ATTITUDE AND WRITINGS ARE VERY DAMAGING. GO BACK TO SAN FRANCISCO OR NEW YORK OR WHEREVER YOU CAME FROM AND LEAVE THE NATIVES BE.

WE ARE ALL NATIVES OF THE LAND ON THIS SPACESHIP EARTH. IF YOU, AS A NATIVE, FIND THAT YOUR LAND HAS BEEN USURPED BY THE RICH ANGLOS, WHO CAN YOU HOLD RESPONSIBLE BUT YOUR FELLOW NATIVES WHO FIRST OWNED THE LAND? IT'S TRUE THAT THE ANGLOS TRICKED, TRADED, AND TARGETED THE TRUE NATIVES OF THIS LAND, THE INDIANS, BUT THAT'S THE NATURE OF LAND ACQUISITION ON THIS EARTH. WHEN IT COMES TO THE MORE RECENT SPANISH-AMERICAN NATIVES, I DON'T THINK THEY CAN HOLD THEMSELVES BLAMELESS FOR THE ANGLO INVASION. MONEY TALKS, SURVIVAL MAKES US LISTEN. THE BLAME GOES TO THIS SYSTEM THAT DEMANDS HUMANS EXIST BY THE SAME LAW OF SURVIVAL THAT THE ANIMALS OF THE JUNGLE DO. SURELY WE HAVE GRADUATED BY NOW AND ARE READY TO HELP EACH OTHER, VIA OUR SOCIETAL STRUCTURES, TO HAVE WHAT WE NEED FOR SURVIVAL, SO THAT WE CAN GET ON WITH EVOLUTION OF THE HIGHER BRAIN AND CREATIVE HUMAN

PURPOSE. YOU WANT THE ENCHANTMENT OF THE PAST, AS THINGS WERE WHEN THEY WERE STILL YOURS. I WANT THE ENCHANTMENT OF THE FUTURE, WHERE A NEW APPROACH TO LIFE SEEMS POSSIBLE. BOTH OF US ARE DISSATISFIED WITH WHAT WE HAVE TO DEAL WITH IN SOCIETY NOW. WE WOULD PROBABLY AGREE WITH EACH OTHER, WERE WE TO SIT AND TALK OVER COFFEE.

■

GALISTEO NEWS, SANTA FE, N.M.

WHY AREN'T PEOPLE OUTRAGED WITH THE STATE OF OUR PLANET, AND WHY AREN'T WE GROUPING TOGETHER TO DO SOMETHING ABOUT IT?

MANY OF US ARE OUTRAGED, BUT THE ODDS OF GROUP- ING TOGETHER IN THE EXPRESSION OF THIS OUTRAGE ARE AS GREAT AS THE DIVERSITY OF OPINION ON *HOW* TO DO SOMETHING ABOUT IT. WE WHO ARE OUTRAGED ARE MORE RUGGED INDIVIDUALS THAN WE ARE JOINERS. THEN, TOO, FEAR ENTERS. THE POLITICIANS WHO OUTRAGE US HAVE LOTS OF AUTOMATIC WEAPONS AND MEGABUCKS TO MOUNT AN UNBEATABLE WAR ON THE OUTRAGED, TO INFILTRATE AND DEFUSE THEIR OPPOSITION. I COUNT ON MOTHER NATURE TO DO THE OUTRAGEOUS WORK OF CRACKING AND FISSURING THE WORLD AS WE KNOW IT.

THE GAMUT, SANTA FE, N.M.

HOW CAN I GROW UP TO BE
A REAL PRINCESS?
(Asked by Amber, seven years old)

BY ALWAYS REMEMBERING THAT YOU WANT TO BE A
PRINCESS; BY DOING A LOT OF RESEARCH, READING,
INVESTIGATION OF WHAT A PRINCESS HAS BEEN IN THE
PAST AND WHAT A PRINCESS IS TODAY. A TRUE PRINCESS
GLOWS JOY FROM HER HEART, IS LOVING, KIND, AND COM-
PASSIONATE TOWARD PEOPLE, IS NOT STUCK-UP OR VAIN
ABOUT BEING A PRINCESS OR BEING PRETTY OR BEING
SPECIAL. A TRUE PRINCESS USES HER VERY NICE POSITION
IN LIFE TO HELP OTHERS WHO ARE NOT SO FORTUNATE.

THE GAMUT, SANTA FE, N.M.

WHAT SHOULD I DO WHEN THE BOMBS DROP—PRAY FOR MY SINS, OR GET LAID, OR WHAT?

FIND WHERE THE EPICENTER OF THE BOMB DROP WILL BE, GATHER YOUR NEAREST AND DEAREST CHUMS, AND GO WITH THEM TO THAT EPICENTER. SIT IN YOGIC POSTURE, IN A CIRCLE, HOLD HANDS WITH THE PEOPLE ON EITHER SIDE OF YOU, AND CHANT YOUR FAVORITE CHANTS. CHANTING THE MANY NAMES OF ESSENCE WILL CAUSE YOUR SOUL TO GRAVITATE TOWARD INFINITE REALITY AS THE NUCLEAR EXPLOSION FISSIONS THE SOUL'S MOLECULAR STRUCTURE, DISINTEGRATES THE EGO, AND TAKES YOU TO NIRVANA, READY OR NOT.

■

GALISTEO NEWS, SANTA FE, N.M.

WHY DO SO MANY PEOPLE OVER THIRTY LET THEIR BODIES GO TO HELL?

BODIES HAVE MORE FUN IN HELL—YOU KNOW THAT!

THE VILLAGE VOICE, N.Y.C.

IS LIFE BETTER IN MIAMI?
BETTER THAN WHAT?

ONLY THE COCKROACHES ARE BETTER IN MIAMI, BETTER AND BIGGER THAN IN NEW YORK. AND WOULD YOU BELIEVE, THEY FLY!

■

GALISTEO NEWS, SANTA FE, N.M.

WHAT IS MOST IMPORTANT NOW?

HUMOR, RELEASE, TEARS; FACING DARKNESS, SWIMMING THE ABYSS STRONGLY TILL THE SHORE IS REACHED, BEING WITH YOUR EXPERIENCE. BOTH TEARS AND LAUGHTER ARE HEALING. LAUGHTER, SCIENTIFIC EXPERIMENT RECENTLY DISCOVERED, HAS THE SAME EFFECT ON THE BODY AS AEROBIC EXERCISE, AND CRYING SPEEDS UP THE HEALING OF WOUNDS. WE MAY NOT FEEL ABLE TO HEAL THE WORLD, BUT WE EACH HAVE THE TOOLS TO HEAL OURSELVES.

GALISTEO NEWS, SANTA FE, N.M.

CAN A NATION LIKE THE ITALIANS, WHO HAVE ELECTED A PORNO QUEEN TO THEIR PARLIAMENT, BE ONTO SOMETHING?

THE ITALIANS HAVE ALWAYS BEEN ONTO *GUSTO* IN EVERY-THING THEY DO. I THINK THE PORN QUEEN WILL DEMON-STRATE A HEART FOR THE UNDERDOG AND AN EXPERIENCED EYE FOR THE HYPOCRISY OF THE PRE-TENDERS TO MORAL AND FISCAL RESPONSIBILITY.

■

GALISTEO NEWS, SANTA FE, N.M.

WHAT DO YOU DO WHEN ALL EMOTION, MEANING, AND FEELING GET LOST IN GEOMETRY, SPACE, AND ENERGY?

EAT A CHEESEBURGER, RARE, AND CHASE IT DOWN WITH A BEER.

HUDSON STREET PAPERS, N.Y.C.

RESPONSE TO REQUEST FOR A POEM, AND THE QUESTION: WHERE IS THE SILENCE ON HUDSON STREET?

THE RIVER OF HUDSON STREET

FLOWS NOISE

TOOTS HORNS

SCREECHES WHEELS

BUZZES LIGHTS

WHOOSHES TAXIS

GROWLS BUSES

JABBERS PEOPLE—

WHERE IS THE SILENCE ON HUDSON STREET?

WHERE IS THE SILENCE ON ANY STREET

OF THE MIND?

WHERE IS THE SILENCE

PERIOD?

THE COSMIC NOISE IS ALL THE SILENCE

WE GET

THE UNIVERSAL *HUMMMMOHMMMM*

FOUND BETWEEN

JABBER GROWL TOOT AND SCREECH

BETWEEN

IS FOUND THE SILENCE ON HUDSON STREET

ON ANY STREET

OF THE MIND.

THE GAMUT, SANTA FE, N.M.

IS THERE LIFE AFTER FIFTY?

YES, YES, A MILLION TIMES YES: THERE'S MORE VIVID LIFE THAN EVER. THE FIFTIES ARE FREEDOM TIME (5 IS A NUMBER OF EXPERIENCE AND FREEDOM). TURNING FIFTY IS LIKE BEING GIVEN A MEDAL OF HONOR FOR TIME WELL SERVED. BEING FIFTY ENTITLES YOU TO BE LOOKED TO FOR WISDOM. BEING FIFTY GIVES YOU THE OPTION OF BEING FOXY VAMP OR WOMAN-AS-PERSON, OR ALTERNATING THE TWO AT WILL; AT WILL BECAUSE THE GROINAL NEED HAS SUBSIDED. BEING FIFTY ENTITLES YOU TO BE A TANTRIC TEACHER OF SENSUAL DELIGHT. AND TODAY, THERE IS MORE YOUTH AVAILABLE AT FIFTY THAN EVER BEFORE: WE'VE BEEN LIVING WITH MORE VIM AND LESS DRUDGERY FOR A FEW DECADES, AND IT'S CATCHING UP WITH US.

VERY SPECIAL ARTS, ALBUQUERQUE, N.M.

WHY ARE SOME PEOPLE PERFECTIONISTS?

WE ARE TAUGHT TO REGARD THE END RESULT AS MORE IMPORTANT THAN THE PROCESS. MOST PEOPLE OBEY THIS SAD TEACHING AND HATE THEIR LIFE, WHICH THEY SPEND PRETENDING TO BE MORE THAN THEY'RE REALLY UP TO BEING. WE HAVE TO LET GO OF BEING PERFECT AND GET HOLD OF *BEING*.

■

THE GAMUT, SANTA FE, N.M.

IS IT PROPER TO BUY WEDDING PRESENTS WHEN IT STATES "NO GIFTS PLEASE" ON THE INVITATION?

IF THE GIFT COMES FROM YOUR HEART, NOT FROM YOUR SENSE OF OBLIGATION, THEN THE ACTION IS RIGHT. *PROPER?* THE ROOT OF THE WORD "PROPER" IS THE LATIN *PROPRIUS*, "ONE'S OWN, PERSONAL." SO YES, IT'S *PROPER* INDEED TO BUY THE GIFT IF IT'S FROM YOUR OWN TRUE HEART.

THE·VILLAGE VOICE, N.Y.C.

WRITE ABOUT HOW LIFE IS IN THE JOINT.

MEAN. VIOLENT. INHUMAN. ZOO. PRISON IS THE WORST EXPERIENCE OFFERED ON THIS DIFFICULT EARTH; PRISON AND INSANE ASYLUMS. PRISONS TURN HUMAN BEINGS INTO VIOLENT HYENAS. PRISON REFLECTS THE LIMITS OF HUMAN EVOLUTION THUS FAR. PRISON IS A HATE FACTORY.

■

GALISTEO NEWS, SANTA FE, N.M.

WHEN THE WORLD IS TIRED AND THE SKY IS CRYING, WILL THE BIRDS BE SINGING STILL AS THE HUMANS STAND SILENT?

THEN, ONLY THE WIND WILL SING.

■

THE VILLAGE VOICE, N.Y.C.

WILL THERE EVER BE A THIRD WORLD WAR? IF THERE IS, TIME, PLACE, LOCATION, AND WHERE CAN I GO TO LIVE WITHOUT GETTING MY BALLS BLOWN OFF?

IT HASN'T BEEN DECIDED YET, BUT IF THERE IS, GO WHER-EVER YOUR SENSE OF RIGHT-BEING LEADS YOU, SURELY SOMEWHERE IN THE COUNTRY OR MOUNTAINS. OF COURSE, IF IT'S YOUR KARMA TO GO, GO LONGING FOR THE AFTERLIFE, NOT CLUTCHING TO THIS ONE, AND YOU'LL HAVE A SMOOTHER PASSAGE.

INTERNATIONAL WOMEN'S FORUM, SANTA FE, N.M.

CAN YOU REMAIN NONVIOLENT IN THE CONFLICT WITH A VIOLENT ADVERSARY AND SURVIVE?

PERHAPS. GANDHI DID, FOR A LONG WHILE. BUT HIS SUR-VIVAL WAS FRAUGHT WITH JAIL AND MANY BEATINGS. HE SURVIVED BECAUSE HE HAD A SENSE OF ETERNITY ABOUT SURVIVAL. HE BELIEVED IN THE SOUL'S CONTINUED EXIS-TENCE. NONVIOLENCE—WITHIN YOURSELF IS WHERE IT BEGINS—IS VERY DIFFICULT TO ACHIEVE. EARTH EXISTENCE IS ITSELF A VIOLENT ADVERSARY, AND EVERY DAY WE HAVE TWELVE OR SO STRUGGLES TO ACHIEVE A NONVIOLENT RESPONSE. MOST OF US SURVIVE THESE FOR SIXTY YEARS OR MORE.

■

THE GAMUT, SANTA FE, N.M.

WHAT IS THE ROOT OF INSANITY?

NO, NO, NO TO THE WORLD!

SHAKESPEARE & CO., N.Y.C.

WHEN WILL I MAKE IT?

WHEN YOU'VE PERSEVERED LONG ENOUGH, OVERCOME ENOUGH HURDLES TO MEND OR ERADICATE YOUR FLAWS; WHEN YOU'VE HIT BOTTOM AND FEEL YOU'LL NEVER BE ABLE TO GET UP AGAIN, THEN FIND THAT THE MOST INTERESTING CHOICE IS TO BEGIN ANEW; WHEN YOU OPEN YOUR HEART TO YOURSELF AND TO LIFE AND TO YOUR WORK, NOT TO MENTION TO YOUR FELLOW HUMAN BEINGS, AND MAYBE EVEN TO A LOVER. AFTER ALL, WHAT IS "MAKING IT"? WHAT DID YOU WANT TO MAKE, MONEY OR HARMONY?

■

CARDS & SUCH, FOREST HILLS, N.Y.

HOW DO YOU SET A GOAL AND STICK TO IT?

WANT IT! DESIRE IS THE SUPREME FUEL.

■

THE VILLAGE VOICE, N.Y.C.

WHY DO I SOMETIMES THINK THAT MY LIFE HAS NOT YET BEGUN?

BECAUSE YOU HAVEN'T STARTED TO LIVE YOUR *TRUE* LIFE. YOU'RE TOO BUSY STRUGGLING FOR SURVIVAL.

THE GAMUT, SANTA FE, N.M.

WHY DO DOGS ALWAYS SEEM CONTENT?

IF YOU WERE TREATED LIKE A LITTLE GOD, PETTED, PLUFFED, FED, WALKED, ALL CARES TAKEN CARE OF, WOULDN'T YOU BE CONTENT? MAYBE A DOG'S LIFE IS A COSMIC REWARD FOR TIME WELL SERVED IN HUMAN FORM.

■

HUDSON STREET PAPER, N.Y.C.

HOW DO INCENSE MAKERS MAKE INCENSE?

SOURCES INFORM ME THAT INCENSE IS MADE FROM COW DUNG, WHICH IS SOAKED IN PRECIOUS, PLEASANTLY ODORIFEROUS OILS, THEN LEFT TO DRAIN UNTIL THE EXCESS OIL DRIPS OFF. FROM COW DUNG TO SWEET SMELL—QUITE AN ALCHEMICAL WORK, ONE THAT CARRIES THROUGH IN ITS HOUSEHOLD FUNCTION.

■

GALISTEO NEWS, SANTA FE, N.M.

WITH THE BERLIN WALL DOWN, I CAN'T HELP BUT WONDER: WHY DIDN'T PEOPLE SNAP EARLIER? WHY DID SO MANY TEARS HAVE TO FALL BEFORE IT CAME DOWN?

IT TAKES A LOT OF TEARS TO MELT THE HEART OF POWER.

GALISTEO NEWS, SANTA FE, N.M.

SHOULD I PURSUE ACTING AS MY CAREER?

IF YOU LOVE IT, PURSUE IT.

IF YOU LOVE IT MORE THAN THE SECURITY AND PLEA-SURES MORE STABLE LIVELIHOODS CAN BRING, PURSUE IT.

IF YOU FEEL FROM THE DEEPEST YOU TO THE OUTERMOST YOU THAT YOU ARE AN ACTOR—THAT IS, THAT YOU HAVE THE CAPACITY AND DESIRE TO TAKE ON MANY OTHER PER-SONAS, TO FIND YOUR SELF THROUGH THESE OTHER PERSONAS, TO UNDERSTAND LIFE THROUGH UNDER-STANDING THE SITUATIONS THESE PERSONAS ARE INVOLVED IN:

IF YOU ARE THIS PERSON, THEN YOU DO INDEED LOVE ACTING MORE THAN MONEY AND ITS PLEASURES, AND YES, DO THEREFORE ALWAYS PURSUE THIS ACTION OF DRAMA-TIZING HUMANITY'S FOLLY AND BEAUTY; AND KNOW THAT YOU'RE HELPING US ALL BY LIVING YOUR TALENT.

THE VILLAGE VOICE, N.Y.C.

DOES NICENESS REALLY COUNT?

IT SURE MAKES THE DAY SWEETER!

■

GALISTEO NEWS, SANTA FE, N.M.

ISN'T SELLING AN ART FORM?

ANY WORK DONE WITH WHOLE-BEING JOY IS A FORM OF ART. ART IS WORK MADE FUN AND FUN MADE WORK.

■

ZIA DINER, SANTA FE, N.M.

WHY DOES IT SEEM THAT THE PEOPLE WHO HURT OTHERS HAVE IT EASIER FINANCIALLY?

THE BUSINESS OF ACCUMULATING MONEY IS WAGED BY THE RULES OF WAR: SO THOSE WHO ARE MOST FIERCE AND CALLOUS RULE THE MONEY MARKET. (BUT WHEN IS THE WORLD WHERE WE VALUE CREATIVE LIVING MORE THAN BULGING BANK ACCOUNTS?)

INTERNATIONAL WOMEN'S FORUM, SANTA FE, N.M.

HOW CAN THE BICYCLE BECOME A MORE VIABLE MEANS OF TRANSPORTATION? CAN IT?

MAJORITY RULES, AT LEAST IN AMERICA. A MAJORITY OF FOLKS WILL HAVE TO *WANT* TO SAVE ENERGY AND GAIN VITALITY BY RIDING THEIR BICYCLES TO WORK. THIS MAJORITY WILL THEN HAVE TO SPEND THEIR OWN ENERGY AND TIME BOMBARDING LOCAL GOVERNMENTS TO CREATE BICYCLE ROADS ALONG THE MAJOR THOROUGHFARES. IN THE MEANWHILE, SET THE EXAMPLE: RIDE YOUR BIKE, INVITE YOUR FRIENDS TO TRY THE EXPERIENCE FOR A WHILE. OFFER THEM SOMETHING IF THEY ARE RELUCTANT: PROVIDE THE BIKE, OFFER TO BABY-SIT OR COOK DINNER. GETTING AMERICANS TO GIVE UP THEIR COMFORTABLE CRUISING CARS IS NO EASY TASK. CONVINCING ANYONE OF ANYTHING TAKES A GREAT CONVICTION ON YOUR PART, GREAT ENOUGH TO SEE YOU THROUGH A LONG, ARDUOUS EFFORT.

GALISTEO NEWS, SANTA FE, N.M.

WHY IS A HANGOVER CALLED A HANGOVER?

BECAUSE IT WAS OBSERVED, BACK IN THE EARLIEST DAYS OF CIVILIZATION, THAT WHENEVER THE IMBIBING OF TOO MUCH LIQUOR OCCURRED, THE FOLLOWING MORNING USUALLY SENT THE DRINKER OUT TO THE TERRACE, WHERE HE (IN THOSE DAYS, USUALLY A HE) WOULD HANG OVER THE RAILING AND EMPTY HIS STOMACH OF THE POISONOUS CONTENTS DRUNK THE NIGHT BEFORE. THUS WAS THE TERM "HANGOVER" COINED FOR THE MORNING AFTER THE NIGHT OF TOO MUCH.

■

SHAKESPEARE & CO., N.Y.C.

COULD YOU PLEASE DEFINE
"ARTIST" FOR ME?

AN ARTIST IS ONE WHO SEES EVERY MOMENT OF LIFE AS A CREATIVE WORK.

THE GAMUT, SANTA FE, N.M.

DO I HAVE ANY CHANCE AT ALL OF ATTAINING PEACE IN THIS PHYSICAL WORLD IF I CONTINUE TO ESCHEW A CAREER?

A CAREER IS THE VEHICLE THAT DRIVES YOUR INNATE PURPOSE ALONG THE COURSE OF LIFE. WHY DO YOU ESCHEW SUCH A VEHICLE AS A CAREER? WHAT ELSE IS THE LIFE WELL LIVED BUT A CAREER? NOW, YOU MUST MAKE A LIVING, YES? DO YOU WANT TO MAKE A LIVING AT SLAVE LABOR, SO TO SPEAK, WORKING FOR IDIOTS WHO WANT NOTHING BUT REGIMENTATION FROM YOU? OR DO YOU WANT TO MAKE YOUR LIVING VIA THE SMOOTH FLOW OF DOING WHAT YOU LOVE TO DO? SUCH IS THE OPTIMUM RENDITION OF "CAREER," THE ROOT MEANING OF WHICH IS: FROM THE FRENCH *CARRIERE*, RACECOURSE; FROM MEDIEVAL LATIN *CARRARIA*, ROAD FOR VEHICLES; FROM LATIN *CARRUS*, A KIND OF VEHICLE.

HUDSON STREET PAPERS, N.Y.C.

WHY AM I IN BUSINESS SCHOOL?

BECAUSE YOU'RE GIVING IN TO THE COMMERCIAL SOCIETY INSTEAD OF FOLLOWING YOUR HEART'S WORK. IF YOU CAN'T CONSIDER THE WORK YOU DO TO BE YOUR PARTIC- ULAR BEST EXPRESSION, YOU'RE IN THE "WRONG" LINE AND NOT PARTICIPATING IN "RIGHT LIVELIHOOD." IN AMERICA, IT TAKES ABOUNDING COURAGE TO PURSUE THIS RIGHT LIVELIHOOD, HENCE IT'S THE ACTIVITY MOST NEEDED AT THIS TIME. HOW OFTEN DO YOU ASK YOUR- SELF, WHY AM I IN BUSINESS SCHOOL?

■

THE GAMUT, SANTA FE, N.M.

SHOULD I USE MY TALENT WHEN I GROW UP, OR BE WHAT I WANT TO BE?

BEING WHAT YOU WANT TO BE *IS* USING YOUR TALENT!

HUDSON STREET PAPERS, N.Y.C.

WHAT IS THE BEST WAY TO CELEBRATE A HOLIDAY (YULE, HANUKKAH, CHRISTMAS, SATURNALIA, BEETHOVEN'S BIRTHDAY, ETC.)?

GIVE

FROM THE HEART

RATHER THAN THE POCKETBOOK. (NOW, IF YOUR HEART

OPENS YOUR PURSE JOYFULLY, THAT, TOO, IS GIVING FROM

THE HEART.)

GIVE

A SMILE

A TOUCH

A DOLLAR

TO THE HOMELESS.

GIVE A PHONE CALL

TO SOMEONE YOU KNOW IS ALONE.

MAKE A GIFT

FOR YOUR FRIEND OR A STRANGER,

COOK A BREAKFAST FOR YOUR FAVORITE PERSON.

GIVE RECOGNITION TO THE BLISSES OF LIFE: WHILE

YOU'RE WALKING,

LOVING, EATING, RELIEVING, BREATHING.

AND MOST OF ALL, GIVE YOURSELF APPRECIATION.

THESE ARE THE BEST WAYS TO CELEBRATE EXISTENCE,

AS WELL AS

CHRISTMAS AND BEETHOVEN'S BIRTHDAY.

LOOKING GLASS BOOKSTORE, PORTLAND, ORE.

NOTE LEFT BY WINDOW READER:
KNOWING THAT
A HUMAN IS
MIND-BODY-SOUL
AND THAT A SOUL
IS IMMORTAL
CHANGES ONE'S
POLITICS

NON SEQUITURS

THE VILLAGE VOICE, N.Y.C.

HOW DOES
A DESERT
LAUGH?

DRYLY,

WITH CACTUS

FLOWERS

AND THE

CURLING SMILE

OF ARROYOS.

HUDSON STREET PAPERS, N.Y.C.

DO YOU THINK HIMALAYANS ARE
UNATTRACTIVE WITH THEIR TEETH PULLED?

IT DEPENDS IN WHICH DIRECTION THEY'RE PULLED. IF IT'S TO THE WEST, THEY TEND TO LOOK SLEAZO, LIKE A HARLEM PIMP. IF THEY'RE PULLED TO THE SOUTH, THEY'RE APPEARING ON THE SWEATY SIDE; IF THE TEETH ARE PULLED TO THE NORTH, HIMALAYANS TEND TO LOOK SHRIVELED. BUT IF THE TEETH ARE PULLED TO THE EAST, HIMALAYANS LOOK MAGNIFICENT, THEIR MYSTICAL, DEMON-RESPECTING NATURE IS MAGNIFIED, AND THEIR COLORFUL CLOTHING BRIGHTENS THEIR TOOTHLESS GRIN.

■

GALISTEO NEWS, SANTA FE, N.M.

IF YOU WERE A FLOWER, WOULD YOU
RATHER BE PICKED OR PLUCKED?

BEING PLUCKED ASSURES BEING TOUCHED.
BEING PICKED CAN OFTEN BE ONLY AN IDEA.

THE VILLAGE VOICE, N.Y.C.

I'VE HAD MY UNDERWEAR ON FOR THREE MONTHS. MY FRIENDS SAY CHANGE THEM. WHAT DO YOU THINK?

WHY GIVE IN TO YOUR FRIENDS' DEMANDS? LIVE THE LIFE OF THE HERMIT. MAKE DIRT YOUR BEST FRIEND AND BODY ODOR YOUR CONSTANT AND ONLY COMPANION.

■

HUDSON STREET PAPERS, N.Y.C.

TOPIC SUGGESTION: OYSTERS

THOUGH SLIMY, OYSTERS ARE CREATIVE, TRANSFORMATIONAL CRUSTACEANS. THEY TURN GRIT INTO GEMS AND HAVE GAINED A HUGE REPUTATION FOR INDUCING SEXUAL PROWESS IN HUMANS. PERHAPS THIS IS BECAUSE THEY DO NOT USE SEXUAL ENERGY FOR THEIR OWN PURPOSES; THEY PROCREATE IN A MORE ETHEREAL MANNER THAN THE ANIMAL HUMAN, HENCE STORE UP SEX ENERGY. OYSTERS ARE A HERMETIC BUNCH AND SPEND THE MAJORITY OF THEIR TIME ALONE, IN THEIR SHELLS, CREATING PEARLS OF BEAUTY, IF NOT WISDOM. THEIR SHELLS THEMSELVES, AT THE OYSTERS' DEMISE FOR THE PURPOSE OF SLIPPING DOWN HUMAN THROATS, ARE QUITE UTILITARIAN, SERVING AS RECEPTACLES FOR THE BURNING ASHES OF THE SMOKE STICKS THAT BRING MANY HUMANS TO AN EARLY END.

GALISTEO NEWS, SANTA FE, N.M.

IS THE LEGEND OF ELOY GARCIA TRUE?
PLEASE ELABORATE.

AH, THE INFAMOUS ELOY GARCIA,* THE LOS ALAMOS LETCH. ACCORDING TO THE LEGEND, ELOY GARCIA HAD A CUSHY JOB IN THE LOS ALAMOS LABS A DECADE AGO; THOUGH ON WEEKENDS, HE'D LET IT ALL HANG OUT, PLAYING IN HIS BAND, ELOY GARCIA AND THE ROADRUNNERS. TROUBLE IS, BY DAY, ELOY HELD ALL THE FEMALES WHO WORKED FOR HIM IN THE THRALL OF TERROR: IF THEY WANTED TO GET AHEAD, THEY HAD TO GIVE HEAD. ELOY IS RUMORED TO HAVE KNOWN EVERY CLOSET IN THE LITTLE LAB HE RULED, AND HE MADE GOOD USE OF THEM OFTEN DURING THE DAY, FOR TEN-MINUTE FLIGHTS OF FELLATIO FERVOR. ELOY'S HAREM FUNCTIONED SMOOTHLY FOR YEARS, UNTIL THE INEVITABLE DAY WHEN COMEUPPANCE DELIVERED ELOY TO KARMA. A NEW FILE CLERK WAS DOWN ON HER KNEES IN ONE OF ELOY'S FAVORITE CLOSETS, HER MOUTH FILLED WITH ELOY'S FLAMING SPEAR, WHEN SUDDENLY THE POOR GIRL HAD AN EPILEPTIC FIT, CAUSING HER TEETH TO CLAMP DOWN HARD AND FAST ON THAT SPEAR, UNTIL THE MEDICS GOT THERE TEN MINUTES LATER. ELOY'S NOT BEEN HEARD OF SINCE, NOR HAVE THE ROADRUNNERS. AND NOBODY'S HEARD ANY RUMORS ABOUT WHETHER OR NOT ELOY'S SPEAR STILL FLAMES.

*THE STORY IS TRUE, THE NAMES HAVE BEEN CHANGED.

GALISTEO NEWS, SANTA FE, N.M.

IF HONESTY IS THE BEST POLICY, WHAT'S THE SECOND BEST?

SILENCE.

■

CARDS & SUCH, FOREST HILLS, N.Y.

WHERE DOES THE SETTING SUN GO AFTER ITS GONE DOWN?

IT GOES TO THE GREAT FURNACE UNDER THE HORIZON, WHERE THE SUN ANGELS CLEAN OUT THE ASHES THAT HAVE COLLECTED DURING THAT DAY AND THROW DEW ON THE CHURNING FLAMES TO QUIET THEM DOWN FOR A NIGHT'S SLUMBER. AT THE STROKE OF 4 A.M., THE MORNING CREW OF SUN ANGELS ARRANGE THE LOGS FOR THAT DAY'S BURNING, LIGHT THE KINDLING, AND BLOW UPON THE FLAMES UNTIL THE FIRE'S ROAR IS SUITABLE FOR THE TEMPERATURE OF THE SEASON. WE HAVE WINTER BECAUSE SO MANY SUN ANGELS TAKE THEIR VACATION IN THOSE MONTHS.

VERY SPECIAL ARTS, ALBUQUERQUE, N.M.

**WHERE DO RAINBOWS GO AT NIGHT? CAN
YOU ANSWER THAT FOR ME? I HOPE SO!**
(Asked by a six-year-old girl)

RAINBOWS GO TO THE OTHER SIDE OF THE WORLD, TO
BRING MAGIC TO THE ORIENTALS AND GIVE THE CHINESE
AND JAPANESE WOOD FAIRIES SOMETHING TO DO. WHAT
DO THEY DO? THEY POLISH THE GOLD PIECES AT THE END
OF THE RAINBOW AND MAKE SURE THAT ALL THE RAIN-
BOW COLORS ARE SHINING BRIGHTLY. THEY USE DEW, BY
THE WAY, TO WIPE THE RAINBOWS CLEAN.

■

THE GAMUT, SANTA FE, N.M.

HOW DO RIVERS GET THEIR RAPIDS?
(Asked by an eight-year-old girl)

BY RUNNING AROUND THE ROCKS THAT GET
IN THEIR PATH.

GALISTEO NEWS, SANTA FE, N.M.

CANNED GOODS
BIRDS OF PREY
LAWN FURNITURE
VELCRO
SAFE SEX
THE INDUSTRIAL REVOLUTION
YOUNG REPUBLICANS . . .
OK?

CANNED GOODS ARE GOOD ONLY AFTER THE

HOLOCAUST, WHEN ANY NOURISHMENT IS NEEDED.

BIRDS OF PREY ARE EXQUISITE FIERCE FREE FLIERS,

HONEST IN THEIR KILL AND CARING.

LAWN FURNITURE IS TOO UNCOMFORTABLE AND

UNSTABLE TO MAKE LOVE ON.

VELCRO FLIES: HAVE THEY COME INTO STYLE YET? WHAT

A GREAT ROAR OF A RIP!

SAFE SEX IS PASSION MUTATING.

THE INDUSTRIAL REVOLUTION STARTED PIECEWORK AND

THE DEATH OF PRIDE-IN-WORK: HOW MUCH PRIDE CAN

YOU TAKE IN MAKING THE HEAD OF A NAIL THAT YOU'LL

NEVER SEE, AND DOING IT DAY AFTER DAY?

YOUNG REPUBLICANS ARE FOOLING THEMSELVES, BUT

NOT US.

OK?

HUDSON STREET PAPERS, N.Y.C.

CAN A VEGETARIAN EAT A SHMOO?

SHMOOS ARE BEINGS WITH CLOUD BODIES AND THERE-FORE IMPOSSIBLE TO *EAT*. ONE CAN *IMMERSE* IN THE DEW OF A SHMOO, AND ONE CAN INHALE SCHMOO. THESE SHMOO JOYS ARE PLEASURABLE TO VEGETARIANS AND MEAT-EATERS ALIKE; THOUGH A VEGETARIAN WOULD TEND TO HAVE A GREATER TASTE FOR SHMOO IMBIBING, SINCE VEGETABLE-EATERS ARE MORE SENSITIVE THAN MEAT-EATERS. AND YOU, QUESTIONER, MUST BE AS ANCIENT AS I AM, TO REMEMBER SHMOOS, AL CAPP'S LOVING, PURRING FORERUNNERS TO TRIBBLES!

■

HUDSON STREET PAPERS, N.Y.C.

WHY DO ZEBRAS HAVE BLACK STRIPES INSTEAD OF WHITE?

MY UNDERSTANDING IS THAT THEY HAVE *WHITE* STRIPES ON A *BLACK* BODY. THEY ARE, AFTER ALL, AN AFRICAN ANIMAL, AND METAPHYSICAL LEGEND HAS IT THAT THE WHITE STRIPES FORETOLD THE INTRUSION OF THE WHITE MAN IN THE BLACK HUMAN'S LIFE.

VERY SPECIAL ARTS, ALBUQUERQUE, N.M.

WRITE ABOUT TERMINAL DESPAIR.

TERMINAL DESPAIR IS LOCATED IN THE SMOGGY INDUSTRIAL TOWN OF MONEYOLA, GONEAWRYLAND, ANYWHERE IN THE WORLD. IT'S A LONG WAIT FOR THE TRAIN OF FLIGHT THAT TAKES YOU OUT, WITH OPIATES OF MANY KINDS FOR REFRESHMENTS. NOR IS THE READING MATERIAL OF ANY HELP; YOU CAN PERUSE MINIMAL ESSAYS ON VIOLENCE IN SEX, IN THE HOUSEHOLD, IN NATIONS, IN MACDONALD'S, IN RELIGION, EVEN IN COOKERY (THE TOO VARIOUS RECIPES FOR THE PREPARATION OF SUCH AMERICANISMS AS JELLO & OKRA SALAD OR TOMATO ASPIC WITH TUNA AND MARSHMALLOWS). HOWEVER, THERE ARE REPUTED TO BE, HIDDEN IN OCCULTED NICHES WITHIN TERMINAL DESPAIR, ORAL, SYNAPSULAR TEACHINGS THAT, ONCE FOUND AND DIGESTED, PROMISE TO GIVE THE RECEIVER ASTRAL FLIGHT TO ANY OF THE SUNNIER, MORE HUMANE, WORLDS OF THE UNIVERSE. I HAVE FOUND A FEW OF THESE NICHES MYSELF, SOME OF WHICH BLESSEDLY LEAD TO KNOWLEDGE OF HOW TO SWIM THE ABYSS AND COME UP CREATING.

GALISTEO NEWS, SANTA FE, N.M.

WHAT IS THE ANSWER TO THE FISH'S
QUESTION "WHY IS THERE AIR?"

THE WHITECAPS IN THE MOONLIGHT, THE BIRDS WHO
SLEEP BETWEEN THE WAVES.

■

SHAKESPEARE & CO., N.Y.C.

WHAT IS THE DIFFERENCE BETWEEN A DUCK?

THERE IS A DUCK THAT GLIDES GENTLY OVER THE LAKE
WATERS; AND THERE IS THE DUCK OF ITS HEAD AS IT DIPS
ITS BILL INTO THE LIQUID FOR REFRESHMENT. ON CON-
SULTING MY FRIENDLY DICTIONARY, I FIND THERE IS ALSO
DUCK CLOTH, "A VERY DURABLE, CLOSELY WOVEN HEAVY
COTTON OR LINEN FABRIC," AND THE MILITARY TRANS-
PORT DUCK, "AN AMPHIBIOUS MILITARY TRUCK USED
DURING WORLD WAR II."

THE GAMUT, SANTA FE, N.M.

WHY DO CAMELS SPIT AND HAVE HUMPS,
WHILE LLAMAS JUST CHEW GRASS?

EVERYONE KNOWS THAT LLAMAS ARE SPIRITUAL, THAT THEY HAVE UNDERGONE MUCH TRAINING IN THE HIGH MOUNTAINS OF TIBET AND KNOW HOW TO MIND THEIR MANNERS! CAMELS, ON THE OTHER HAND, HAVE BEEN NOTORIOUSLY PROMINENT IN AMERICA; THROUGH THEIR ASSOCIATION WITH CANCER-PRODUCING INHALATIONS, THEY HAVE INHERITED GREAT, SPEWING, RASTY-NASTY PERSONAS. AS FOR CAMELS HAVING HUMPS, THIS GOES BACK TO THEIR PARTNERSHIP WITH MACHISMO MALES OF YORE, WHOSE PREDILECTION FOR FAST GROINAL RUBS WAS, THROUGH TIME, PROJECTED ONTO THEIR MOST-USED ANIMAL AS THE HUMP ON THE CAMEL'S BACK.

■

VERY SPECIAL ARTS, ALBUQUERQUE, N.M.

WHY IS THE SKY BLUE?

THE SKY ARTISTS THOUGHT BLUE WOULD BE A LOVELY COLOR TO LOOK AT ALL DAY LONG, ESPECIALLY WHEN LYING ON THE GROUND AND GAZING UP THROUGH THE LACY GREEN LEAVES. THEY GOT THE COLOR BY MIXING CHEMICALS TOGETHER. IT'S *YOUR* JOB TO ASK YOUR SCIENCE TEACHER *WHICH* CHEMICALS.

GALISTEO NEWS, SANTA FE, N.M.

WHERE DID THE COLOR GREEN COME FROM?

GREEN IS THE NAME OF THE MOST PROLIFIC OF THE CHIL-
DREN BORN FROM THE MARRIAGE OF ATMOSPHERE AND
LIGHT.

■

THE GAMUT, SANTA FE, N.M.

DO YOU THINK THE EGG WOULD FEEL BADLY IF IT KNEW ITS FATE WERE TO BE MERELY "SCRAMBLED"?

TO THE EGG, BEING SCRAMBLED IS AKIN TO A HUMAN'S
BEING FAMOUS. ANY EGG CAN BECOME A CHICKEN, BUT
TO BE USED FOR HUMAN NOURISHMENT *BEFORE* THE PAIN
OF LIVING ENSUES IS THE HIGHEST HONOR A CHICKEN
AND ITS EGG CAN BE PAID. THE MANNER IN WHICH THE
EGG IS PREPARED FOR HUMAN NOURISHMENT IS IMPOR-
TANT IN DETERMINING THE DEGREE OF GRACE BEING PAID
THE EGG. FRIED, WHETHER SUNNY-SIDE OR OVER EASY, IS
AKIN TO A BRONZE MEDAL; POACHED, A SILVER; WHILE
THE GLORIOUS, THICK, CREAMY SCRAMBLE GETS THE
GOLD MEDAL OF HONOR. THIS IS THOUGHT TO BE SO
BECAUSE HUMANS THEMSELVES ARE SO SCRAMBLED, AND
EMULATION IS AN EGG'S DELIGHT.

GALISTEO NEWS, SANTA FE, N.M.

CAN WE MAKE TIME STAY, LIKE A DOG?

NO, BUT YOU CAN MAKE IT FLY, LIKE A BIRD; OR CRAWL,

LIKE A SNAIL. AND YOU CAN DEFINITELY MAKE TIME, LIKE A

DOG, HEAL.

■

THE GAMUT, SANTA FE, N.M.

WHAT'S THE DIFFERENCE BETWEEN
A BABY AND A ROCK?

SILENCE.

■

THE VILLAGE VOICE, N.Y.C.

WHAT IS YOUR DEFINITION
OF A KNUCKLEHEAD?

ONE WHOSE MIND IS GNARLED WITH IGNORANT

STUBBORNNESS.

GALISTEO NEWS, SANTA FE, N.M.

WRITE A LOVE LETTER FROM
A BURNING BUILDING.

DEAREST BIRDS:

I AM LEAVING YOU NOW, AND FIERCELY SO, WITH A PRAYER THAT I DO NOT DAMAGE YOUR SWEET WINGS WITH THE FLAMES THAT LEAP FROM MY RAFTERS, NOR SUFFOCATE YOU WITH MY SMOKE. I WANT YOU TO KNOW BEFORE I AM CRISPED HOW I LOVE YOU, HOW I HAVE ENJOYED YOU THROUGH MY WINDOWS IN THIS HALF CENTURY—YOUR GENTLE CHIRPING, YOUR MILD BICKERING OVER THE SEEDS MY TENANTS LEFT FOR YOU FROM TIME TO TIME. AND I APOLOGIZE FOR THE THOUGHTLESSNESS OF THESE LAST WHO INHABITED ME AND SO CARELESSLY LET ME BURN. I AM GRATEFUL THAT I CAN SEND THIS NOTE TO YOU WITH THEIR PARROT, WHO HAS THE INTELLIGENCE TO FIND A WAY OUT OF ME BEFORE MY FLAMES SOAR TOO HIGH. AND SO GOODBYE, BIRDS WHO HAVE DELIGHTED ME, AND WORLD THAT HAS AT LAST DISCARDED ME.

WITH LOVE,

THE HOUSE BY THE WILLOW TREE

GALISTEO NEWS, SANTA FE, N.M.

JUST WHAT ARE PINKIES (AS IN FINGER) FOR?

FOR PICKING,

FOR PRESSING "C" AND "F" ON A SAXOPHONE,

FOR STICKING OUT WHEN DRINKING TEA AND COFFEE,

FOR PRESSING "A," "Q," "Z," AND "?" ON THE TYPEWRITER,

FOR SMOOTHING WRINKLES UNDER THE EYE AND

SMUDGING EYELINER,

FOR BRUSHING THE EYEBROWS,

FOR MOCKING THE EFFETE,

FOR BRINGING THE SUM TOTAL OF FINGERS TO FIVE.

■

HUDSON STREET PAPERS, N.Y.C.

HOW ARE THINGS IN GLOCCA MORRA?

LESS GREEN AND GLORIOUS THAN THEY USED TO BE. THE
LEPRECHAUNS HAVE ALL MOVED TO THE DESERT, AND THE
SHAMROCKS HAVE BEEN GROWING ONLY TWO LEAVES IN
THE LAST DECADE. HOWEVER, GLOCCA MORRA ISN'T
TOTALLY WITHOUT LITTLE PEOPLE. I HEAR THERE ARE
SOME TINY ALIENS WHO'VE SETTLED THERE AND ARE
PAINTING SHAMROCKS ALL OVER THEIR SPACE PODS IN
PREPARATION FOR THE REST OF THE WEE GALACTIC FOLKS'
IMMINENT ARRIVAL.

GALISTEO NEWS, SANTA FE, N.M.

WRITE ABOUT THE USE OF JELL-O
IN A CAREER CHOICE.

TO USE JELL-O TO HELP IN THE CHOICE OF A CAREER, ONE MUST PREPARE ONLY *LIME* JELL-O (A GENERIC BRAND OF GELATIN DESSERT CAN BE USED, BUT THE FLAVOR MUST BE LIME; THE LIME-GREEN GELATIN CORRESPONDS IN COLOR TO JELL-O'S PLANETARY RULER, NEPTUNE). POUR THE STILL-LIQUID JELL-O INTO A ROUND GLASS BOWL. ONCE THE JELL-O IS JELLED, IT WILL RESEMBLE A SHIMMERING, SHAKING CRYSTAL BALL. TAKE YOUR SHIMMERING BOWL INTO A SACRED PLACE—THE BATHROOM, WITH CANDLES AND INCENSE, WILL DO—AND SIT IN A COMFORTABLE MEDITATIVE POSITION WITH THE JELL-O BALL IN YOUR LAP OR ON A TABLE IN FRONT OF YOU. PLACING BOTH HANDS AROUND THE BOWL, CLOSE YOUR EYES AND SILENTLY IMPLORE JELL-O'S GUARDIAN PLANET, NEPTUNE, OR ANY ANGEL YOU FEEL FRIENDLY WITH, TO HELP YOU WITH YOUR CAREER CHOICE. BE SURE TO GIVE ALL THE DETAILS, BECAUSE NEPTUNE TENDS TO BE FORGETFUL AND ANGELS DON'T HAVE A FIRM GRASP ON THE DETAILS OF REALITY. NOW OPEN YOUR EYES AND GAZE INTENTLY INTO THE SHIMMERING GELATIN. YOU CAN SHAKE THE BOWL A LIT-TLE TO RUN THE SPIRIT OF YOUR PRAYER THROUGH IT IF YOU FEEL AN ANSWER IS SLOW IN COMING. CONTINUE

THIS GAZING UNTIL THE LITTLE GREEN JELL-O DAKINI EITHER APPEARS IN THE MIDST OF THE JELL-O OCEAN OR WHISPERS THE ANSWER INTO YOUR MIND. IF THE JELL-O MELTS BEFORE THIS HAPPENS, START OVER THE NEXT DAY. DO NOT REPEAT THIS RITUAL MORE THAN THREE TIMES, HOWEVER. IF YOU DO, THE JELL-O DAKINI WILL TRICK YOU INTO GETTING A LOUSY JOB FOR LOTS OF PAY.

■

GALISTEO NEWS, SANTA FE, N.M.

DO ILLITERATES COMPREHEND THE FULL IMPACT OF ALPHABET SOUP?

YES, BUT SYMBOLICALLY. ILLITERATES SEE IN ALPHABET SOUP AN EXQUISITE MOSAIC THAT SCREAMS THE SENSORY MESSAGE "NOURISHMENT."

■

GALISTEO NEWS, SANTA FE, N.M.

WHAT HAPPENS TO "ERASED" WORDS?

THEY CHANGE INTO PARTICLES OF RUBBER AND LEAD, WAFT TO THE GROUND, AND GET SWEPT AWAY INTO COR-NERS OR FERTILE FIELDS. THEY ARE NOT GONE FOREVER, THOUGH, THESE ERASED WORDS. THEY LEAVE THEIR IMPRESSION ON THE TABLET THEY WERE WRITTEN ON.

GALISTEO NEWS, SANTA FE, N.M.

WHY ARE THERE ZEBRAS?

LONG AGO, IN A TIME NOW FORGOTTEN, THERE LIVED IN AFRICA'S SERENGETI A POWERFUL KING, WHO SUFFERED FROM A STRANGE ABNORMALITY. HALF OF HIS SKIN WAS WHITE, THE WHITE OF A REDHEAD'S SKIN, THE WHITE OF AN ALBINO; AND THE OTHER HALF WAS EBONY BLACK. POWERFUL AS HE WAS, THIS ABNORMALITY PLAGUED THE KING'S MIND AND MOOD. ONE DAY, HE CALLED HIS COURT WIZARD TO HIM. "WIZARD," HE BOOMED, NOT EVEN OFFERING THE WIZARD PERMISSION TO RISE FROM HIS PROSTRATE BOW. "I WANT YOU TO USE YOUR POWERS TO PASS ON MY COLORING TO ALL THE CITIZENS OF MY KING-DOM." NATURALLY, THE WIZARD AGREED, FOR A GREAT PART OF HIS MAGIC WAS HIS ABILITY TO GET ALONG WITH THE KING. BUT THE WIZARD WAS AS WISE AS HE WAS SLY, AND THIS REQUEST TROUBLED HIM SO MUCH THAT HE DECIDED TO TAKE A WALK IN THE PROVERBIAL DESERT, WHERE WORDS OF WISDOM WERE SCATTERED IN THE DUNES. LOOKING UP AT THE SKY, THE WIZARD CALLED ON THE PARTICLES AND WAVES, KNOWN TO HIM THEN AS GOD, AND CRIED: "GOD, WHAT SHALL I DO WITH THIS OUTRAGEOUS ORDER? I CANNOT SO DISSERVE MY LIEGE AS TO TURN HIS SUBJECTS INTO SUCH MONSTROSITIES THAT THEY WILL RISE AGAINST HIM, YET I CANNOT DIS-

OBEY." THE PARTICLES REPLIED IN A VOICE THE WIZARD NAMED "THE ANGEL": "WIZARD, HAVE WE GOT A DEAL FOR YOU. THERE'S A TRIBE OF BEASTS WE JUST CREATED, AND THEY'RE NOT WORKING OUT. WE CALL THEM DON- KEYS. WE'LL SEND YOU THE FIRST BATCH, AND YOU CAN CHANGE THEM INTO WHATEVER YOU WANT." SUDDENLY THERE APPEARED BEFORE THE WIZARD A TROOP OF DON- KEYS, OR SO THE WIZARD, WHO'D NEVER SEEN A DONKEY BEFORE, SURMISED. CALLING ALL HIS ENERGIES TO THE POINT BETWEEN HIS EYES, HE BREATHED IN DEEPLY, RAISED HIS ARMS BEFORE HIM, POINTED HIS FINGERS AT THE HERD, AND FORCEFULLY THRUST THEM FORWARD, RELEASING A WILD, FEROCIOUS "SHAZAM!" BEFORE HIS VERY AMAZED EYES, THE ANIMALS' COLOR CHANGED FROM MUD BROWN TO EXQUISITE BLACK AND WHITE STRIPES. SINCE THE KING'S NAME WAS ZEBRAD, THE WIZARD NAMED THE NEW CREATURE "ZEBRA," KNOWING THIS WOULD FLATTER THE KING AND CAUSE HIM TO ACCEPT THIS SWITCH IN PLANS. AND INDEED HE DID, AND RULED COMPASSIONATELY OVER HIS KINGDOM FOR TWENTY MORE YEARS BEFORE HE PASSED IT ON TO HIS SON. FOR THE LAST TWO YEARS, HE RODE THE SERENGETI ON HIS PET ZEBRA, LEADING THE SMALL HERD THAT WAS THE ROYAL ZEBRA'S FAMILY TO WHAT WOULD BE THEIR MUTUAL ROYAL BURIAL GROUND.

LOOKING GLASS BOOKSTORE, PORTLAND, ORE.

HOW HAPPY ARE CLAMS, ANYWAY?

AS HAPPY AS YOU WOULD BE IF YOU WERE LOCKED AWAY FROM THE WORLD BY CHOICE IN THE COZINESS OF YOUR OWN SWEET, WARM LITTLE WORLD, WITH ALL YOU NEEDED RIGHT AT YOUR BECK AND CALL, KNOWING THAT IN YOUR COMFORT, YOU WERE DOING WHAT YOU WERE MEANT TO BE DOING.

■

HUDSON STREET PAPERS, N.Y.C.

WHY DO FISH SWIM?

IT'S EASIER THAN TREADING WATER.

■

GALISTEO NEWS, SANTA FE, N.M.

JOAN OF ARC BURNS IN SPIRITS OF FLAME, BURNING STILL; WHEN I BURN, WILL I BURN WITH HER BURNING WITHIN EVERY VEIN?

WHEN THE SPIRITS OF FLAME LICK THE SOUL, THE BURN-ING IS EVER THE SAME BURNING, AS JOAN KNOWS AND AS THE TAPASYA-ENGULFED SAINTS KNOW, AND IT SEARS ALL THE VEINS OF BLOODY HOPE. WE ARE BURNING NOW; SAINT JOAN IS NEAR.

STAGHORN, N.Y.C.

TOPIC SUGGESTION: WINTER DOLDRUMS

IN THE WINTER, THE MOOD TURNS AS GRAY AS THE SKIES, AND THE SOUL CONTRACTS WITH THE COLD. PERUSAL OF ONE'S LIFE ENSUES, THOUGHTS OF WHAT THE FUTURE HOLDS OR DOESN'T HOLD. IF ONE IS ALONE IN THE WINTER, THE HEART ACHES FOR WARMTH OF CUDDLES AND "THAT SPECIAL" COMPANIONSHIP. WINTER DOLDRUMS ARE EASED BY THE AMBER GLOW OF A FIRE IN THE FIREPLACE, BREAD BAKING IN THE OVEN, GREEN CHILI STEW SIMMERING ALL DAY ON THE STOVE, DINNER AND A BOTTLE OF WINE WITH FRIENDS, BRANDY AFTER SKIING (OR HOT BUTTERED RUM), AND A FAT, FASCINATING NOVEL TO CUDDLE UP WITH UNDER THE ELECTRIC BLANKET. WINTER IS THE TIME MYSTICS SAY THE SUN AND THE SOUL MOVE NORTHWARD, THE TIME TO EXAMINE THE PAST AND PLAN THE SPRING'S BLOSSOMING. DOLDRUM IS DEFINED AS "A PERIOD OF INACTIVITY, LISTLESSNESS, OR DEPRESSION" AND IS DERIVED FROM THE WORDS "DULL" AND "TANTRUM." WINTER DOLDRUMS, THEN, SPEAK OF DULL TANTRUMS OF DEPRESSION. SKI, DANCE, LOVE, OR READ THEM OUT OF YOUR WINTER, OR YOUR SKIES WILL BE COLDER AND GRAYER THAN NATURE'S.

GALISTEO NEWS, SANTA FE, N.M.

WHEN DO YOU CALL A SPADE A SPADE?

WHEN YOU'RE FAMILY, MAN, AND ONLY THEN!

■

GALISTEO NEWS, SANTA FE, N.M.

IS COCK ROBIN A BIRD OR A CRIME?

ACTUALLY, COCK ROBIN IS A NAME COINED IN MASSAGE PARLORS IN THE SEVENTIES. IT WAS THE NAME GIVEN FOR AN EXTRACURRICULAR MASSAGE, WHICH WAS SPRUNG UPON THE CLIENT BY SURPRISE AS AN ATTENDANT MADE OFF WITH HIS WALLET. IT IS ALSO A MODERN TERM FOR AN ANCIENT ROMAN RITE OF PASSAGE AMONG YOUNG MALE MILITARY OFFICERS.

■

SHAKESPEARE & CO., N.Y.C.

WHAT IS THE COLOR OF RAIN?

RAIN IS THE REFLECTION OF ALL COLORS OF THE WORLD, THE MIRROR OF ONE'S MOOD. RAIN IS LOVELIEST IN PUR-PLE, HAPPIEST IN SUNSET PEACH, GAYEST IN YELLOW, AND MOST MYSTICAL WHEN GLISTENINGLY INVISIBLE SILVER.

GALISTEO NEWS, SANTA FE, N.M.

**WHAT IS THIS OBSESSION ABOUT LICKING
ONE'S INDEX FINGER BEFORE TURNING A
PAGE? WILL THE ACIDS IN SALIVA
EVENTUALLY CAUSE THE EDGE OF THE PAGE
TO DETERIORATE MORE RAPIDLY?**

NOT MORE RAPIDLY THAN THE CHEMICALLY TREATED PAPER
WILL CAUSE THE FINGER-LICKER TO DETERIORATE!

THE GAMUT, SANTA FE, N.M.

**WRITE A STORY ABOUT A TEENAGE BOY
WHO'S ACTUALLY A SWEDISH PRINCE WHO
WAS ADOPTED BY A FAMILY FROM WHITE
BEAR LAKE, MINNESOTA, WHEN HIS PARENTS
WERE KILLED IN A FREAK
MOTORBOAT ACCIDENT.**

JOHN FELT NO GRIEF AFTER HIS PARENTS WERE KILLED.
THEY WERE COLD, UNFEELING PEOPLE, SUBJECT TO THE
DEEP DEPRESSION THAT CLOUDED MOST OF SWEDEN'S
CITIZENS. HE'D GROWN TO LOVE HIS ADOPTED FAMILY
LONG BEFORE THE ACCIDENT. HE'D VISITED THEM EVERY
SUMMER FOR MOST OF HIS SIXTEEN YEARS, AND NOW
THAT HE WAS STARTING TO FEEL THE PULSING OF SPRING,
HE FOUND HIMSELF MOVING CLOSER, IN A MORE PASSION-
ATE WAY, TO THEIR SEVENTEEN-YEAR-OLD DAUGHTER. OF
COURSE, HE NEVER RODE IN MOTORBOATS ANYMORE. THE

ACCIDENT THAT ENDED THE LIVES OF HIS ROYAL PARENTS HAD IMPLANTED A PERMANENT FEAR OF SPEED ON THE WATERS. INSTEAD, HE TOOK HER FOR LONG WALKS UNDER THE FLOURISHING MINNESOTA TREES. THERE, AT THE EDGE OF WHITE BEAR LAKE FOREST, JOHN AND JILLIAN WOULD SIT FOR HOURS, DISCUSSING HOW THEY WOULD TRANS-PORT THE SWEDISH PRINCE'S ROYAL HOLDINGS TO MIN-NESOTA. HE WAS AN AVID COLLECTOR OF SWEDISH SUICIDE PARAPHERNALIA, AND HIS COLLECTION OF PAINT-INGS, NEWS CLIPPINGS, AND SUICIDE NOTES WAS MOST PRECIOUS TO HIM. IT WAS TRULY A KISMET MATING FOR JILLIAN AND THE YOUNG PRINCE, FOR THIS SPRINGTIME GIRL WAS HERSELF AN AVID COLLECTOR, NOT OF SUICIDE MEMORABILIA BUT OF PUNK BUTTONS, POSTERS, AND ALBUM COVERS. NOT OF THE MUSIC. THE MUSIC, SHE TOLD THE PRINCE, DIDN'T SOUND LIKE MUSIC TO HER, WHICH MADE HER LOVE PUNK MUSICIANS EVEN MORE, FOR DAR-ING, AND SUCCEEDING ON PURE STYLE. AS IT TURNED OUT, TO MAKE THIS THE SHORT STORY IT NEEDS TO BE, THE PRINCE AND JILLIAN WERE HAPPILY MARRIED, AND THEIR COLLECTION OF SUICIDE NOTES AND PUNK ART WAS THE BASIS FOR ONE OF MINNESOTA'S MOST POPULAR MUSEUMS IN THE TWENTY-FIRST CENTURY, THE MUSEUM OF ARMAGEDDONAL HISTORY.

STAGHORN, N.Y.C.

AND THE QUESTION NO ANSWER CAN DO JUSTICE TO:

HELP! WHO ELSE CAN I ASK BUT YOU! CAN A THIRTY-TWO-YEAR-OLD ANGLO-GAELIC WOMAN ARTIST CONTINUE A YEAR-OLD RELATIONSHIP WITH A TWENTY-FOUR-YEAR-OLD ITALIAN REAL ESTATE BROKER (A WOMAN) WHO RECENTLY BECAME ENGAGED TO A TWENTY-SEVEN-YEAR-OLD UKRAINIAN AIR-CONDITIONING RETAILER (A MAN) AND FIND HAPPINESS?